"I've never forgotten you, Eve," Adam said softly.

"That kiss last night, it wasn't an impulse. I wanted to kiss you from the minute I saw you at the shelter. My big hit, 'Impossible to Forget,' I wrote that song because of you."

Eve swallowed. She wanted to look away, but she couldn't. Even when he reached for her hand, her gaze remained glued to his. When he gently pulled her toward him, h̶̶̶̶̶ nd even though her ̶̶̶̶̶ *No! Stop! Don't d̶* w her into his arms.

"I want you, Eve."

She closed her eyes as his lips grazed her cheek and drifted down to her neck.

"I've always wanted you," he whispered.

Every nerve ending in her body seemed to be alive with sensation. And when he raised his head to capture her mouth, she moaned, and instead of stopping him, she kissed him back as if her very life depended upon it...

* * *

THE CRANDALL LAKE CHRONICLES:
Small town, big hearts

Dear Reader,

I have always been fascinated by books dealing with themes centered around the road not taken. And one day, while listening to a love song written by a current pop star, the idea for *The Girl He Left Behind* began to form, quickly becoming an idea I couldn't ignore. In fact, it seemed perfect for book two of The Crandall Lake Chronicles.

I had tons of fun revisiting Crandall Lake and writing Adam and Eve's story. I hope you enjoy reading it as much as I loved writing it and that you'll look for the next book in the series (coming in August 2016), which will tell Olivia's story.

I love to hear from readers. Come and visit me on my website at patriciakay.com.

Happy reading!

Patricia Kay

The Girl
He Left Behind

—

Patricia Kay

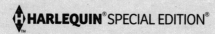
HARLEQUIN® SPECIAL EDITION®

Recycling programs
for this product may
not exist in your area.

ISBN-13: 978-0-373-65954-8

The Girl He Left Behind

Copyright © 2016 by Patricia A. Kay

This edition published by arrangement with Harlequin Books S.A.

For questions and comments about the quality of this book, please contact us at CustomerService@Harlequin.com.

® and TM are trademarks of Harlequin Enterprises Limited or its corporate affiliates. Trademarks indicated with ® are registered in the United States Patent and Trademark Office, the Canadian Intellectual Property Office and in other countries.

Printed in U.S.A.

Formerly writing as Trisha Alexander, **Patricia Kay** is a *USA TODAY* bestselling author of more than forty-eight novels of contemporary romance and women's fiction. She lives in Houston, Texas. To learn more about her, visit her website at patriciakay.com.

Books by Patricia Kay

Harlequin Special Edition

The Crandall Lake Chronicles
Oh, Baby!

The Hunt for Cinderella
Holiday by Design
Meet Mr. Prince
The Billionaire and His Boss

Callie's Corner Café
She's the One
It Runs in the Family

The Hathaways of Morgan Creek
You've Got Game
His Best Friend
Nanny in Hiding

Visit the Author Profile page
at Harlequin.com for more titles.

This book is dedicated to Dick,
with whom I shared fifty-three years of adventures.
We all love and miss you!

"There is a charm about the forbidden that makes it unspeakably desirable."

—*Mark Twain*

Prologue

The boy stands under the overhang, guitar case in hand, his backpack stuffed with his belongings. The bus will arrive any minute. Beyond the overhang the rain falls steadily. It has been raining for days here in the Texas Hill Country.

His gaze sweeps the station platform.

Is she coming?

He'd told her she had to be here no later than eight o'clock. The station clock now reads eight twelve. The bus is due to leave the station at eight fifteen. The boy looks at his phone again. Should he risk calling her house? But what if her father answers? For at least the hundredth time since they'd become a couple, he curses her father's stupid rules. Eve is one of the few girls left in their senior class who doesn't yet have a cell phone. He has no way of contacting her without alerting her parents.

He looks around slowly, hoping this time he'll see her, that she'll be out of breath from hurrying, saying how sorry she is that she made him wait, that she didn't say yes when he first started talking about her coming with him, that she made him worry. But she's not there. The only other person on the platform is an older man who was already there when the boy arrived.

She's not coming.

His heart thuds painfully as the truth sinks in. Yet he isn't really surprised. Down deep, hasn't he always known she wouldn't come? That he's never been good enough for her? Hasn't he been lying to himself all along, pretending she would change her mind and come because he didn't want to think about the alternative?

You're on your own. She doesn't love you enough to defy her family. You knew she wouldn't leave home. It was never gonna happen. Forget about her. The two of you together was always a fairy tale, and you've never believed in fairy tales.

He thinks about how he'd once told Aaron to grow up, saying, "There ain't no Santa Claus, kid, and you might as well get used to it!"

He sighs. Yeah, there ain't no Santa Claus. And there sure as hell wasn't gonna be a happy ever after for him. Not with Eve anyhow. He'd have to make his own happy ever after by making his dream of a career in music come true.

The hiss of air brakes heralds the arrival of the bus, and the boy pulls his baseball cap more firmly on his head and darts through the rain toward the opening doors.

Two minutes later, as the bus pulls away from the station, heading east toward his future, the boy gives one last, long look at the town where he's spent all eighteen years of his life so far.

Then he turns resolutely away. No more looking at the past. From now on, he will only look forward.

Chapter One

Twelve years later...

Eve Kelly stared at the headline.

Adam Crenshaw and Version II Launching Fall
Tour in Austin

She could hardly believe her eyes.
Adam.
Adam was finally coming home. He would be per-
forming in Austin. Which was less than an hour away.
Eve swallowed while the enormity of what she'd just
read in the online version of the *Austin American-
Statesman* sank in.

Twelve years. It had been twelve years since the day
Adam had ridden out of her life. Twelve years to won-

der if she'd done the right thing or if her long-ago decision had been the worst one she'd ever made.

She sighed heavily. Read the accompanying story quickly. There wasn't a whole lot of information, just the fact that Adam Crenshaw and his band would be opening their North American tour in Austin at the Frank Erwin Center the first week of September, and that tickets would go on sale next month. The reporter also mentioned that this would be the first time Adam's band had performed in Texas even though he had grown up in Crandall Lake. There was a photo of the band with Adam front and center, but it had been taken from a distance, and his head was bent over his guitar, so she couldn't see his face.

"Time to head out, Eve. You gonna come to Ernie's, have a drink with us?"

Eve started. She hadn't heard Penny Wallace, one of her coworkers, approach. She glanced up and smiled. "Thanks, but I can't. I have to stop at the supermarket, then pick up the twins and take them over to Bill's."

"They spending the week with him?"

Eve nodded. "Yeah."

"Okay. See you on Monday."

After Penny walked off, Eve shut down her computer and gathered her things. Her head was still full of the startling news about Adam, but she couldn't sit here and think about it, nor could she call her cousin Olivia to tell her the news. Not if she wanted to get the twins to her ex's by six thirty, as promised.

Fifteen minutes later, she strode into her favorite supermarket and headed straight into the produce department. She was having Olivia for dinner the following night and needed fresh salad stuff. She also wanted to be sure to send some fruit with the twins tonight. Maybe she couldn't compete with Missy, their stepmother, as far as baking cakes and pies from scratch, but she could make sure the twins had plenty of fresh fruit while they were there.

The market was crowded, but Eve knew exactly what she needed and where to find it, so within twenty minutes she was standing in the checkout line. She'd chosen the shortest line, but there were still two people ahead of her. Friday nights were always so busy. People stopped in after work rather than have to make a separate trip later or the following day. Idly, she glanced at the magazine rack to her left while she waited. And did a double take as she saw the newest issue of *People* magazine.

The cover screamed Sexiest Man Alive! Adam Crenshaw!

And there was a head shot of Adam, smiling out at her, taking up the entire cover, and looking even handsomer than normal. She swallowed painfully as she took in his shining, longish brown hair and unusual gray eyes. His face bore a fashionable stubble, and the dimple in his left cheek was prominently displayed by his sexy, crooked smile. For years, ever since Adam had become successful, people had compared his good looks to another country idol, Keith Urban, but Eve thought Adam was even better looking. She knew Nicole Kidman would probably disagree with her. But then, both of them had to be prejudiced.

Eve grabbed the top copy of the magazine and furtively put it into her shopping cart. She knew she was asking for heartache, but she couldn't resist reading about Adam's life. Reading about all the things she could have had and had rejected.

The two of you would probably have split up by now.

Eve closed her eyes, but the words in her head wouldn't go away. It was stupid to speculate on what might have been if she'd made a different choice all those years ago, and yet she couldn't seem to stop herself. Thankfully, before she'd had time to continue with her morose thoughts, it was her turn to check out, and she no longer had time to think about anything other than the task at hand—watching carefully to make sure she wasn't overcharged for anything.

But when the checker scanned the magazine, she grinned, and with a twang that announced she'd probably grown up in East Texas said, "He sure is a hottie, isn't he? And to think he grew up right here in Crandall Lake!"

"Mmm," Eve said.

"So do you know him?" the checker persisted.

Eve frowned. "Me? Uh, no." The last thing she wanted to do was discuss Adam Crenshaw.

"Oh. I thought maybe you were about his age."

Eve shrugged, hoping she'd discouraged the girl.

"I sure would love to see him. He's comin' to Austin, him and his band. Did you know that?"

Eve forced a smile. "No, I didn't." *Please just finish checking me out and stop talking!*

Finally the girl ran out of steam and a few minutes later, Eve was out of the store and loading her groceries into her car. Resolutely, she pushed every last thought of Adam out of her mind. Time enough to think about him again after the twins were gone tonight. Until then, she would simply be Eve Kelly, mother of Natalie and Nathan, and nothing more.

Adam Crenshaw swore softly. He'd been working on a new song for days and was having problems with the bridge. Nothing he tried sounded right. "Dammit," he said again, frowning and setting his guitar down with a tired sigh. He rubbed his forehead. A headache had been hovering for hours, and he was afraid it was finally going to come. He'd better take some Advil and head it off. His headaches were notorious and could lay him low for days once one took hold.

After gulping down the Advil and pouring himself a glass of iced tea, he picked up his phone and texted his brother.

That contract ready yet?

It only took a moment for Austin's reply.

Yep. Sending in a few mins.

Adam smiled. The money he'd spent on his brother's education hadn't been wasted. Austin was a cracker-jack lawyer and took care of every financial and legal aspect of Adam's career. Adam trusted him more than anyone else in the world.

Turning back to his guitar, he strummed the last few chords before the bridge, hoping for inspiration. And, as happened sometimes, an idea struck, but before he'd had time to get it down on paper, his office door opened and his publicist, Bethany D'Angelo, walked in.

He looked up in annoyance. "Don't you ever knock?" He didn't try to hide his irritation.

She raised her eyebrows. "Aren't *we* in a bad mood today?" Parking her backside on the corner of his desk, she crossed her legs and grinned at him. "Did we get up on the wrong side of the bed, sweetums?"

He gritted his teeth, hating the way she talked in the third person and called him various pet names. She was thirty-one years old, for God's sake, and just because he'd stupidly become sexually involved with her a few months back didn't give her the right to act as if she owned him. This wasn't the first time he'd had the almost uncontrollable urge to fire her on the spot. But he stopped himself in time, and "I have a headache" was all he said.

"Oh, baby, I'm sorry. Did you take something for it?"

"Yes, I took something."

"How about if I rub your shoulders and neck? That'll help, too." She dropped her voice to what she considered her sexy tone. "Then later, I could do something else for you, which I know would make you feel even better."

"I'm having problems with this new song," he said, just as if he hadn't heard her, "and I was just about to have a breakthrough when you interrupted me."

"Oh, you always say you're having problems."

There was something about her airy dismissal of his concerns that nearly pushed him over the edge, but once again, he managed to control himself. Maybe he was being unfair. Just because he was bored with their relationship and wanted out didn't mean he was allowed to act like a total jerk and be nasty to her. After all, she hadn't thrown herself into his bed. He'd made the first move. It wasn't her fault he'd almost immediately known he'd made a huge mistake. So the right thing to do was tell her, straight-out, in a nice way, that from now on their dealings would be strictly business. Then, if she felt she couldn't handle that change in their status, she would quit on her own. If not, they'd go forward as adults.

Forcing his voice into a more pleasant tone, he said, "Did you want something, Bethany?"

"As a matter of fact, I did. I wanted to remind you of your interview with *Rolling Stone* at seven tonight."

"Oh, crap." He had forgotten all about the interview.

"Now, Adam, landing the cover story of *Rolling Stone* is a remarkable coup for you. Coming on top of the *People* thing just a few months before the launch of your tour and a new album… Well, it's fabulous!"

He sighed. "Yeah, yeah, I know. But I hate interviews."

"You've told me that a hundred times. And as I've told *you*, Aaron can't do everything for you. There are some things you simply must do yourself." Gone was the seductress voice. Now Bethany was all business.

In mentioning Aaron, she was referring to the fact that his youngest brother now functioned as Adam's alter ego in matters of publicity, especially his online presence. Aaron, who at twenty-five was five years younger than Adam, pretended to be Adam on Twitter, Facebook, Instagram and Pinterest, in responding to various blogs and fan sites, as well as interacting with his fan clubs.

Adam hated all that garbage. Always had. He didn't hate his fans, of course—he liked meeting them, especially at concerts—but if he spent all his time online and doing interviews, when would he be able to write his music? All he'd ever wanted was to write and perform, not blow his own horn about how great he was. It still amazed him that anyone cared about all that stuff entertainers posted. Hell, Aaron even told Adam's followers what he, Adam, had supposedly eaten for breakfast!

"Yeah, I know he can't," he finally said.

Bethany studied him steadily. "So you won't try to blow off the interview, right?"

"I guess not," he said reluctantly. "But I'll never change my mind that it's the music that counts. Not all this other stuff."

She rolled her eyes. "I'm tired of this old argument, Adam. Yes, the music is important. Of course it is. But having your name and face out there, connecting with all those people who plunk down their money to buy your music and see your shows is equally important. In the long run, maybe even more important. And *Rolling Stone*! I mean, you've arrived. They hardly ever put a country star on their cover. The fact they want you means they consider you a crossover artist, and isn't that what you wanted?"

Before he could answer, his cell rang and he saw it was Austin calling.

"Gotta take this," he said, waving Bethany off.

Accepting the call, he said, "Hey, bro. What's up? Thought you were gonna send over that contract."

"I am. I will. But something's happened," Austin said.

"Oh?"

"Mom's had a heart attack."

"What?" Adam stood. "When?"

Bethany, alerted by his tone, frowned and got off his desk.

"Right after I texted you, she collapsed. I called 911 and I'm riding in the ambulance on the way to the hospital right now. They've got her stabilized but it's pretty serious. I think you need to come."

"Of course. You're *sure* she's gonna be okay?"

"They think so, but we'll see what the docs say when we get there."

"Okay. Keep me posted. I'll try to get out on a flight tonight."

"What?" Bethany said when he hung up. "What do you mean, get out on a flight tonight? You have that interview tonight, Adam!"

"This is more important." He quickly explained what Austin had told him.

Bethany opened her mouth, probably to protest, but closed it again when she saw the look on his face. She sighed wearily. "Okay, I'll call *Rolling Stone* and explain. Hopefully they can postpone the interview for a few days and still make their deadline."

"Don't make any promises. I have no idea how long I'll be gone." Adam was already packing up the stuff on his desk that he wanted to take with him.

"What do you mean? Surely you won't be gone *that* long."

His voice hardened. "I said, don't make any promises. I'll call you when I know my mother's condition."

"I could come with you…" she said hopefully. "I can take care of everything from—"

"It's better if I go alone," he said, cutting her off.

"But—"

Ignoring her, he strode out to the hallway where his secretary, Donna, had a desk. "Donna, get me on a flight to Austin tonight, however you can. And I'll need a rental car when I get there." Unfortunately, his personal plane was down for repairs.

"Okay."

"I'll be upstairs packing. Oh, and get me some cash, too, will you?"

Because he knew she expected it, and because he was in no mood for any kind of scene right now, he told Bethany goodbye, dropped a hasty kiss on her lips and said he'd be in touch.

Then he headed up to his bedroom to begin preparing for his first trip home to Crandall Lake since the day twelve years ago when he'd boarded the bus that had brought him here to Nashville—and success beyond his wildest dreams.

Eve drove slowly home after dropping the twins at Bill's. It was always a wrench to see them leave. Sharing custody with him by alternating weeks was the fairest thing to do, she knew that, but just because it was fair didn't mean she had to love it. She missed the twins when they were gone. Okay, so they were only fifteen minutes away, just on the other side of Crandall Lake, but the truth was, they might as well have been on the moon in comparison to where they lived with her.

After the divorce, Eve had stayed in the starter home she and Bill had bought a few months after they were married. Well, *he'd* bought it. She certainly hadn't had any money to contribute. She was only eighteen and barely out of high school. He was twenty-two and had been working at a good job for almost a year, ever since his graduation from college. The house was a small ranch style with three bedrooms, two baths and an attached garage. The only thing that made it different from its neighbors was the front porch Bill had paid extra to have added because he knew how much she loved having a front porch with a swing. Although the neighborhood was quiet and nice, it wasn't anything special, and it was on the wrong side of town in terms of prestige.

Bill and his new family, on the other hand, lived in the most fashionable part of Crandall Lake, right near the park and the river. Their home was a stately five-bedroom Colonial on a heavily wooded lot. There was a beautiful pool and they even had a tennis court. Bill was an avid tennis player.

Bill's new wife, Melissa, had already given him a child. Will was eleven months old, and the twins were crazy about him. They were crazy about Melissa, too, whom they called Missy. For days, it was "Missy this" and "Missy that" after they'd spent a week with Bill. Their attachment to Bill's new family was a continual source of disquiet to Eve. She worried that because she was a working mother with limited time, and Melissa was a stay-at-home mother who always had lots of time to bake and play with her two and their baby brother, that one day the twins would prefer to live with their father full-time.

How would she handle it if that happened? There was no way she'd agree, of course, but what good would refusing do her if the twins resented her for it? She didn't want them by default. She wanted them to *want* to be with her.

Olivia was always telling her she worried way too

much, that she borrowed trouble, but Eve couldn't seem to help it. She was a worrier, always had been. "Anyway," as she'd told Olivia just last week when they were discussing the scary possibility Eve might be laid off from the paper, "I don't have to borrow anything. Trouble just seems to find me!"

Thinking about the twins and Bill and the whole rumored-layoff thing had pushed all thoughts of Adam Crenshaw out of her mind, but when she arrived home and saw the *People* magazine lying in the middle of her kitchen table, they came rushing back.

Did he ever think about her?

Wonder how she was doing?

Weigh those two little words—what if?

She doubted it. Because he had never, not once in all these years, tried to contact her. And unlike her failed attempts to call him in those early days, it would have been easy for him. After all, she had been here in Crandall Lake the entire time.

Quit torturing yourself. Throw the stupid magazine away. Adam Crenshaw lives in a different world, one you'll never be a part of. And that's the way it was always meant to be. You knew that at the time. You have built a good life here. You need to remember that and stop mooning over what might have been.

The magazine gave a satisfying thud as it hit the wastebasket.

Chapter Two

Donna had gotten him a seat on a red-eye arriving in Austin at one in the morning. As the plane banked, preparing to approach, Adam gazed down at the lights of the city. Although he was tired, he could never sleep while flying.

By the time they landed and Adam picked up his rental car, he knew it would be close to 3:00 a.m. before he arrived in Crandall Lake. Austin had wanted him to stay with him, but Adam didn't like being in someone else's home—he liked his privacy—so his brother had booked a room at the Crandall Lake Inn. Adam couldn't help smiling wryly at the thought of him, a boy from the wrong side of the tracks, the eldest of the "wild Crenshaw boys," actually staying at the posh inn. Of course, it might no longer be posh. He might find it had gone from its long-ago glory to a faded facsimile.

But as he pulled into the driveway of the three-story inn, he saw that it had retained much of its charm. In fact, it still looked elegant and the kind of place that attracted only the best. Adam wondered if he would be considered part of that elite circle now.

"Mr. Crenshaw? Welcome to the Crandall Lake Inn." The young woman at the desk gave him a bright smile, and he could see the excitement in her eyes. "I hope you had a good trip."

He nodded, returning her smile.

"We're so happy you chose to stay with us," she continued as she swiped his credit card and gave him his keys. "Your suite is on the second floor, with a river view."

"Thank you."

Because he had only brought one bag, plus his guitar, with him, Adam turned down the help of the bellman and went up to his suite on his own. When he opened the door, the first thing he saw was the grand piano in the far right corner of the living area, which was large and well lit, with a wide expanse of windows and French doors overlooking the river. He wondered if this was a special suite chosen especially for him. He doubted there'd be many grand pianos at the inn. He was happy to see it. If he ended up having to stay in Crandall Lake for a while, it would help him to have it there. When he was writing music, he preferred to sit at his own piano with his guitar nearby. He would have to remember to thank the manager in the morning.

To the left of the living area, an open door revealed the bedroom beyond. Setting his bag and guitar down, he walked over to the French doors, opened them and went out onto the wide balcony, where there were several wicker chairs and a table as well as potted plants. There was also another door leading into the bedroom beyond. The cool night air felt good, and the musical rush of the water below sounded soothing and perfect for sleeping.

He knew he should hit the sack immediately. He wanted to be at the hospital early in the morning, and he hadn't slept much at all in the past twenty-four hours. But he was wound up and he also knew he wouldn't fall asleep easily. Deciding a hot shower, followed by a glass of brandy from the minibar, might do the trick, he went into the bedroom and began shedding his clothes. First, though, he would text Austin, let him know he'd arrived and see if there was any change in their mother's condition. Austin's answer came within seconds.

Welcome home. Mom sleeping. No change. More tests tomorrow. See you in a.m.

Reassured, Adam headed for the shower. Ten minutes later, standing under the hot spray, he could already feel some of the tenseness leaving his muscles, and he slowly relaxed.

It was going to be interesting, being back in Crandall Lake. For the first time since he'd known he was coming, he allowed his mind to venture into the area he'd unsuccessfully attempted to banish from his thoughts many years ago.

Would he see her?

And if he did, what would he feel?

What *did* he feel?

He remembered how hurt he'd been by her decision.

Her desertion. By the fact she had never tried to contact him afterward. When he'd discovered, a year or so later, that she'd gotten married scant months after he'd left for Nashville, he'd realized how right he'd been. She'd never really loved him. All she cared about was that family of hers. He'd been a fool to ever think otherwise.

Hell, he hoped he *would* see her.

And when he did, he would make it clear to her and anyone else in the vicinity that she meant absolutely nothing to him.

Less than nothing.

And when his mother was out of danger, he would persuade her to come and live with him, or at least to allow him to have a house built for her on his property in Tennessee. Then when he left Crandall Lake this time, he would not be back.

"I have something to tell you, Eve."

Eve looked at Olivia, who sat at the kitchen table, a glass of red wine in front of her. Her tone seemed awfully serious. "Oh? Something happen?" Olivia constantly had problems with her mother-in-law, and lately the problems had seemed to be escalating.

Olivia nodded. "You could say that."

Eve lowered the heat under her spaghetti sauce. "Cryptic doesn't work with me, Liv. You know I suck at mysteries. I never know who dunnit." Satisfied that her sauce would simmer while the pasta cooked, she poured herself some wine and turned to face her cousin and BFF, as the kids would say.

Olivia's expressive brown eyes met Eve's. "I almost

called you yesterday, but decided this was something I had to tell you in person."

Concern. That was what Eve was seeing. She frowned.

"Adam Crenshaw was at the hospital today," Olivia said slowly.

The statement hit Eve like a blow to her stomach. Her mouth dropped open and she stared at Olivia. "A-Adam…is…is *here*? In Crandall Lake?" But he wasn't supposed to be coming to Texas until September. In fact, Eve had planned to tell Olivia about his upcoming concert tour tonight.

Olivia's eyes were soft with sympathy. She was the only one besides Bill who knew about Adam. Eve, in a low moment years ago, had finally told her cousin about him, but Olivia'd been sworn to secrecy. In fact, they never talked about him. Olivia, like Eve, understood it was better not to dwell on things that couldn't be changed.

Eve, shaking inside, sank into the chair across from Olivia. Her cousin reached across the table and took Eve's hand.

"Are you okay?" she said softly.

Eve swallowed. "I guess I have to be, don't I?"

"Oh, hon, I know how you must feel. I'm sorry, but I knew you needed to know."

Eve nodded. Olivia *did* know how she felt. Olivia had been through worse. She'd lost her beloved husband, Mark, four years ago when his helicopter crashed in Afghanistan. Thea, her little girl, had been born after he died. "Wh-what was Adam doing at the hospital?"

"He came because of his mother. She had a heart attack yesterday. Apparently, his brother called him, and Adam came home. He told me he got in late last night."

"You *talked* to him?"

"Yes." Olivia worked the day shift in Registration and Admissions at the Crandall Lake Hospital.

"I thought you said Adam's brother brought her in."

"Yes, she was brought in late yesterday afternoon, after I'd gone home for the day, but several things were left off the admission form, so I went searching for Austin—you know, the brother who's the lawyer. He's the one who filled out the forms. By the time I found him, Adam was there, too."

Eve knew who Austin was. She'd even seen him a few times, but she didn't really know him and had never spoken to him. Crandall Lake was a small town, but not *that* small. People pretty much knew everything of interest or importance that was happening, but not everyone was on speaking terms with everyone else. "Is Adam's mother okay?"

"She will be, according to the doctors, although there are more tests to run. But even if she is, she'll be recuperating for a while, and apparently Adam's going to stay right here in Crandall Lake while she does. In fact, he told me he hopes to bring her back to Nashville when she's well enough to travel. He said he wants her to live with him."

Eve got up to check the pasta while Olivia kept talking. But each word her cousin uttered contributed to Eve's sense of unreality. Was this really happening? Was Adam Crenshaw really here? In Crandall Lake? For the duration of his mother's recuperation? As far as she knew, he had never come back here before. She also knew—courtesy of the very efficient gossip network in Crandall Lake—that he'd taken care of his mother financially once he'd begun to make money, so that she'd never had to work again. And Eve had also heard how Lucy Crenshaw visited her son often. People had speculated about why he never came to Crandall Lake, though, and what they could do to get him to come. His appearance now was bound to create a huge splash.

Oh, God. What if she should run into him? What would she say? Could she manage it and act normal? Or would she fall completely to pieces like that old Patsy Cline song?

"Do you want to know anything else?" Olivia asked after a minute. "Or do you want me to quit talking about this?"

Eve didn't immediately answer. Instead, to give herself time to calm down, she tested a strand of pasta, then turned the burner off and poured the pasta into a waiting colander sitting in the sink. She didn't look at Olivia.

"Eve? You okay?"

"Yes." But she wasn't. She was a mess.

"You sure?"

Eve sighed deeply. Turned away from the sink and met Olivia's eyes again. "How does he look?"

"Want me to say he's really ugly in person? Or do you want me to be honest?"

"Be honest."

"He looks even better than in his photos. Sexy and handsome and charming. But nice. Awfully nice. I can see what you saw in him, Eve. He didn't act like a big star at all. He just seems like a regular guy. A decent, regular guy worried about his mother."

Yes, even at eighteen he'd been all of those things. He'd been many other things, too. Sweet. Reckless. Sensitive. And lonely. He'd always tried to hide his gentler qualities, though. It hurt Eve to think about him, about the way he'd been with her, about how much she'd loved him, and how much she'd wanted to go away with him. That was why she had tried to erase him from her mind, to *not* think about him. But that had always been impossible. And always would be.

"What are you going to do, Eve?" Olivia asked as Eve finally picked up the drained pasta and dumped it into the pasta bowl sitting on the countertop. Absently, she ladled sauce over the steaming spaghetti.

"I don't know. I mean, I probably won't even see him." But her mind was whirling. If he stayed long enough, chances are she *would* run into him. Then what?

"What if he calls you?"

"He won't." Eve put the bowl of spaghetti on the table. Took the casserole dish filled with her signature turkey meatballs out of the microwave where they'd been staying warm and set them on the table, too.

"But what if he *does*?"

Good question. What if he did? Eve sighed heavily. Looked at Olivia. "He won't call me. I'm sure he hates me." She laughed derisively. "If he even remembers my *name*!"

"Oh, Eve, come on. You're being melodramatic."

"No, I'm not. Think about it, Olivia. I let him down terribly. He loved me. I know he did. He wanted me to go away with him. To share his dreams. He even said the M word. In his mind, I would be just one more person he was counting on who had abandoned him."

She fought the tears that threatened. "I've had a lot of years to think about this. At the time, I thought he didn't love *me* enough to stay. But I think the truth is, I didn't love *him* enough…to go."

"And you paid the price," Olivia said softly.

Eve, fighting to keep from crying, nodded. "Yes. I—I made a mistake. I—I was a coward. Afraid to leave my safe world for the unknown."

"You were just a kid."

"I know that."

"So cut yourself some slack." Olivia smiled crookedly. "In his shoes, I would call you. I would be curious. Plus I'd want you to see with your own eyes how successful I was."

"Men don't think that way," Eve said, finally gaining control of her runaway emotions. She went to the refrigerator and removed the salad and cruet of dressing she'd prepared earlier.

"Sure they do."

"No, he won't call me. He won't want to have anything to do with me."

"Okay, have it your way. So he won't call you. But what if you see him somewhere?"

"I don't know." Once all the food was on the table, Eve sat across from her cousin. "I just hope, if I *do* see him, I don't make a fool of myself."

Olivia reached for the spaghetti server. "I'm glad I'm not in your shoes, hon."

Eve reached for her napkin. *I wish I wasn't in them.* The only thing she *did* know right now was that she had a lot to think about, and that she probably wouldn't get much sleep tonight.

Her sins had finally caught up with her.

Twelve years earlier...

Eve kept looking at the clock on her bedside table. It was almost five. Her dad would be home from work any second. The minutes seemed to be going by so fast. Eight o'clock would be here before she knew it. She looked at her closed closet door. Her duffel bag was inside, on the top shelf. If she did go, the only way she could get it outside without her parents seeing it and asking questions would be to throw it out the window.

I can't go. He shouldn't have asked me to. If he really loved me, he'd stay here. He can write his music here.

Eve had gotten home from school early because the graduation practice was over by two o'clock. When she'd left the auditorium, it was raining, and she was glad her dad had told her to drive today. He was so kind that way, always thinking of her well-being. That was the thing Adam didn't understand, because he didn't have that kind of love and concern in his family. Oh, his mother loved him, Eve was sure she did, but Lucy Crenshaw worked two jobs to support her three boys, because her husband had abandoned his family, then been killed a year later. She wasn't home to take care of Adam or his younger brothers. They pretty much had to take care of themselves, and that meant they'd been running wild for years.

What should I do?

Would Adam go without her? Eve couldn't bear to even think that way. He'd said he loved her. Surely he wouldn't leave her. Not after... She abruptly broke off the thought. Her heartbeat quickened just thinking about what she'd let happen last week. Her parents would die if they knew. They would never, not in a million years, believe Eve could do the things she had. Especially not with a boy like Adam Crenshaw. They wouldn't even be able to believe she'd been *seeing* him, *lying* to them. They thought she was perfect. But Eve hadn't been able to help herself. She'd fallen hopelessly in love with Adam from the moment he first spoke to her.

He loves me, too. He won't go without me.

But what if he does? No. That wouldn't happen. Because she couldn't bear it if he left her.

But he swore he was going. If she *did* go—just *if*— her parents would get over it, wouldn't they? They wouldn't hate her forever. It wouldn't be the end of the world, would it?

Just then, breaking into her tormented thoughts, Eve's mother called, "Eve, honey, come help me set the table for supper." Her parents always called their evening meal supper instead of dinner.

"Okay, Mom, coming," Eve called back. *I don't have to decide now. I can wait till after supper when Dad falls asleep in the recliner and Mom is lost in her book.* If she *did* decide to go, it would be easy to sneak her packed bag out then, to pop her head into the living room and say she was going to Walmart to look at some stuff for her college dorm room.

All through supper Eve was on pins and needles, as her mom always said. She could hardly eat because she was now thinking she was going to go. She just couldn't take the chance that Adam would go without her. She couldn't. She loved him too much. She'd *given* herself to him. How could she let him leave her?

On and on her thoughts went until she'd finally persuaded herself that her parents would get over her leaving, especially after Adam became successful, and he and Eve were married, and everything in their life was wonderful—just the way it was supposed to be. Even their names proved they were meant to be together. Adam and Eve. It was destiny.

Finally supper was almost over. Eve pushed her chair back. "I'll wash the dishes tonight, Mom."

"Wait, honey," her mother said, looking at Eve's dad.

Eve turned to her father, who was smiling at her.

"We have something for you, honey," her mom said. "We wanted you to have it tonight so you could wear it tomorrow." She got up and opened a cabinet drawer, the one she called her junk drawer because she tossed in everything that didn't have its own place. Taking out a small box wrapped in gold paper with a gold ribbon, her mother sang softly, "Sunday's child is bonny and blithe and good and gay," as she handed the package to Eve. It was the verse she'd sung to Eve her entire life, because Eve was their miracle child, the child a forty-year-old Anna had despaired of ever having, the wondrous child born on the Sabbath day, a true gift from God.

"Happy graduation, sweetheart," her dad said.

Eve's heart constricted as she slowly removed the paper and opened the box. Inside, nestled in cotton, was a stunning gold heart pendant studded with rubies. "Oh," she said, nearly speechless. "It—it's so beautiful."

"We're so proud of you," her mom said. "And I know it's not your birthstone, but rubies represent love and mean good fortune for the person who wears them. You have an amazing future ahead of you." Her mother's smile said everything she was feeling as she gazed at Eve.

"You'll be the first Cermak to go to college," her dad said. His voice trembled with emotion.

"And to think you won such a wonderful scholarship," her mother said. She reached over and squeezed Eve's hand.

"You're the best daughter anyone could ever have," her dad said. "Never given us one moment's worry."

"And we know you'll keep on making us proud," her mother added tremulously.

Eve's heart felt like a brick in her chest. How could she leave them without a word? How could she disappear on the eve of her high school graduation, abandon them and all they'd done for her and go off with a boy they knew absolutely nothing about, one they didn't even know she was seeing? The shock, the scandal, the disappointment, the unbearable pain would kill them.

Later, in her room, when the clock read 8:00 p.m. and then eight ten and finally eight fifteen and Eve knew the bus was leaving Crandall Lake, she told herself Adam had changed his mind. That he would call her. That the phone would ring any second, and she would snatch it up and call out to her parents that it was for her, and he would say he just couldn't do it. He couldn't leave without her.

Wouldn't he?

Adam spent most of his time at the hospital for the remainder of the week. And late Saturday afternoon, eight days after his mother's heart attack, when her doctor said she could probably move over to the rehab center on Monday, Adam took a relieved breath and grinned at her. "So, Ma, you're going to live."

"We Crenshaws are tough," his mother said softly.

Adam nodded. They *were* tough. Well, hell, they'd had to be. His father, Frank, had been a gambler and a drunk, and he'd abandoned his family when Adam was six, then been killed in a freak amusement park accident a year later. The former Lucy Costa, his unlucky wife, had waited tables by day and cleaned an office building by night to support herself and her three boys. And even then, it was a struggle.

"Heart problems run in my family, though," Lucy added.

"Yeah, I know."

"So you'd better take care of yourself or you'll find yourself in the same boat one of these days."

Adam nodded again. He'd heard this same lecture many times before. In fact, Lucy had gotten on the "good health, take care of yourself" boat every time she'd visited him over recent years.

"I do take care of myself, Ma."

"Really? Do you exercise every day? Do you eat right? I never see you eat anything except pizza."

"I eat all kinds of healthy stuff," Adam protested. "And I work out all the time." But he was mentally crossing his fingers, because he'd been slacking off lately. On both counts.

A few minutes later, Austin, followed by Aaron, entered the room, and Adam, after greeting his brothers and giving his mother a goodbye kiss, told them he was leaving for the day. "I promised Sally I'd drop into the homeless shelter tonight, maybe play some music for the guys there." Sally was a favorite nurse of his mother's and they'd struck up a friendship.

"Need me to come along?" Aaron asked. In addition to all the social media and publicity stuff Aaron did for Adam, he was also Adam's right-hand man and main gofer, both at home and on the road. Adam had initially put him to work because Aaron needed something to keep him on the straight and narrow, but in the past few years Aaron had made himself invaluable, and Adam depended upon him for just about everything he couldn't do himself.

"Nah. I'll be fine. It's only Crandall Lake."

Aaron shrugged. "Okay. But give me a buzz if you need me."

Adam said he would and left. He wasn't worried about needing Aaron. So far the paparazzi had been pretty respectful of his mother's illness and left Adam alone. Except for a few pictures on Instagram and Twitter, they'd found bigger fish to follow. Adam knew all that would change when he returned to his normal life, so he might as well enjoy the peace and quiet while it lasted.

He was looking forward to talking to and singing for the homeless people in the shelter. Except for a really lucky break at the end of his first month in Nashville, he might have ended up in a shelter himself. Down to his last few dollars—he'd even had to chuck his cell phone because he could no longer afford to pay for it— he'd finally gotten a producer to listen to his demo and give him a chance. That same producer had made a ton of money off him in the intervening years, and they'd remained good friends.

As Adam drove to the shelter, he thought about the

songs he'd sing. And afterward, he'd have an early night at the hotel and a good night's sleep. No drama, no groupies, no photographers chasing him.

And absolutely nothing to worry about.

Chapter Three

Eve couldn't sit still. The kids should've come home tonight, but Bill had called early that morning and asked if he could keep them over the weekend because the Kelly family reunion was taking place in San Antonio and he wanted the twins to be there with him. Eve hadn't wanted to agree, but how could she say no?

That was the biggest problem she had with Bill. He was always so reasonable she could never refuse him when he wanted something. Even if he hadn't been reasonable, she owed him. Not that he ever said so, but the knowledge was always there, unspoken, between them.

I rescued you. You owe me.

She knew that was what he was thinking. And why shouldn't he? She was thinking it, too. He *had* rescued her, and she *did* owe him. Even now, after nearly twelve years, she still felt grateful. In fact, she couldn't imagine what her mother would say if she knew. Even thinking about the problem made Eve's heart beat a little faster.

Her mother would never know. That secret was safe. Bill would certainly never tell anyone—it would be the *last* thing he'd ever want people to know—nor would she. They both had a huge stake in keeping their secret safe.

So she'd said yes to this weekend, even though he could have given her more warning. Surely he'd known about the reunion for weeks now. Why hadn't he told her earlier? She would have insisted on keeping the twins last weekend in exchange.

That's probably exactly why he didn't *tell you.*

Eve knew this wasn't a big deal. It was just that she hated weekends on her own. It would be different if she, too, had remarried and had other children, or at least a partner to go places with her. But she hadn't. And the way things looked, she probably wouldn't. After all, to get married meant you needed to be seeing someone, and she had no prospects on the horizon. Crandall Lake wasn't exactly a dating mecca. And even though, at one time, she'd dreamed about moving to Austin or Houston or somewhere with a bigger newspaper, her dream had turned out to be only a fantasy. Bill's business was here. So here she'd have to stay. She could not take the twins from their father.

Olivia had once suggested Eve might sign up for an online dating service.

"I don't see *you* doing that," Eve had said.

"I'm not ready" had been Olivia's quiet answer.

Eve had been immediately sorry for her retort. At

the time, her cousin had been still mourning her husband's death.

"But it would be good for you, Eve."

Eve knew Olivia had been right. Eve *should* be proactive if she didn't want to remain single her entire life. She would be thirty in just a couple of months, and even though thirty wasn't exactly old-maid territory, and lots of women today married later in life, mostly those women had interesting and successful careers. That wasn't true of her. She worked for a small daily paper struggling to keep afloat with dwindling subscriptions and fewer advertisers. In fact, she'd been hearing rumors of layoffs.

Eve sighed, remembering that conversation. What was she going to do with herself this weekend? She was already bored and it was only six o'clock Saturday evening. There was nothing good on television, Olivia and Thea were in Dallas for the weekend and no one else that Eve knew was free. Her own mother was probably busy with a bridge tournament or something. Ironically, Anna seemed to have more of a social life than Eve ever had—or would have.

After another half hour of yawning and attempting to knit—she had learned this past year—Eve shoved the knitting back into the tote that housed her supplies and got up. "I'm going to the shelter," she announced aloud. She'd begun volunteering at Crandall Lake's homeless shelter six months earlier, and she'd found it very satisfying work. She'd even made friends of some of the women there. "Going to the shelter is better than sitting around feeling sorry for myself," she muttered as she prepared to leave, "or thinking about Adam Crenshaw."

She hadn't heard otherwise, so she figured he was still in town. Given the level of interest in their town's biggest celebrity, who had surpassed former pro quarterback Dillon Burke's position as its most famous alumnus, she knew she would have heard if Adam had returned to Nashville.

Thirty minutes later, as she approached the shelter, her spirits had already improved. It always did her good to come here, made her count her blessings and remind her that despite her problems she was extremely fortunate. She shouldn't ever complain, even to herself. Life could always be so much worse—and was for many. She and her children—in fact, her entire family, everyone she loved—was healthy and had a roof over their heads. What more could she ask for?

Vowing to do better, she walked into the building and saw that she had arrived too late to help serve dinner, but not too late to help clean up. Donning an apron, she joined the other volunteers and in short order they'd cleared all the dirty plates and cutlery.

"I guess you heard who's coming tonight," said Julianne, one of the teen volunteers.

Eve frowned. "Um, no. What do you mean?"

Julianne grinned. "Adam Crenshaw! Oh, c'mon. You knew!"

Eve shook her head. Her stupid heart had already started to gallop, just at the sound of his name. "No, I—I didn't. When will he be here?"

"Any minute," Julianne said. "He's going to *sing*!" Her eyes shone with excitement.

Eve looked around wildly. Any minute! Up to now, she'd managed to avoid going anywhere she thought he might be. Oh, God, she had to get out of here. She knew it would look crazy to leave just ten or fifteen minutes after arriving, but she couldn't stay. So what if the other volunteers gossiped about her? They'd forget about her as soon as Adam started singing. She began to remove her apron, but it was already too late, for the entire room started to buzz with anticipation as Adam walked through the dining room doorway.

Eve could feel herself trembling. Olivia had been right. He *did* look better in person. In fact, he looked gorgeous. She took in the black T-shirt with his band's logo on the front, the tight jeans, the worn biker boots, his shining hair, the dimple that appeared as he smiled at the crowd.

An interviewer had once asked why he never wore cowboy boots or cowboy hats. His answer had been that he'd never been a cowboy and refused to pretend he was. "I'm just a musician," he'd said, "who, a lot of the time, likes to write and sing country music."

Adam. His name felt like a prayer.

She couldn't take her eyes off him. But he hadn't seen her. Thank God, he hadn't seen her. Eve knew she couldn't leave without causing a bit of commotion because there were too many people crowded into the room now. It seemed as if everyone who worked there, plus every person who lived there, had jammed themselves into the room.

She watched as he worked the crowd, shaking hands, signing autographs, allowing people to take pictures of him and selfies with him. He'd come a long way from the insecure boy who covered up his loneliness with fierce privacy and a facade of boredom.

"Hello, y'all," he said now. "Thanks for inviting me to come visit and sing for you."

The crowd yelled out their welcome.

Eve managed to maneuver herself to the back of the room while Adam tuned his guitar from the piano near the doors leading to the kitchen. A few minutes later, among cheers of approval, he launched into his signature hit—the first of his records to go platinum— "Impossible to Forget."

"I told myself I didn't care our love was in the past.
I told myself our promises were never meant to last.
But every day, in every way,
I fought heartache and regret,
The truth was there for all to see,
You were impossible to forget."

As he sang, he seemed to be looking straight at her. Eve wanted to look away, but no matter how she tried, she couldn't. She wondered what he was thinking as he sang. She had always wondered if he'd written the song about her. As their eyes locked, she struggled to contain her emotions. When she couldn't, when tears filled her eyes, she knew she had to get out of there. And fast. So as the song finished, she used the boisterous crowd, many of whom jumped to their feet to applaud and call out other song titles they wanted Adam to sing, to hide her exit.

She headed straight for the back door, but when she got there, safely out of sight of the people in the dining room, she discovered it was locked for the night. She was going to have to go out the front. She would have to pass by Adam.

He had begun another song. Best to go now, while he was busy singing. Maybe she could make her escape without too much disturbance. Taking a deep breath, she turned toward the dining room.

About halfway through "Impossible to Forget" Adam realized the attractive blonde he was singing to—he always picked one person in the crowd with whom to have eye contact—was Eve. He hadn't realized it at first because, after all, it had been twelve years since he'd seen her. At seventeen going on eighteen, she'd been wide-eyed, pretty and sweet looking, a girl who wore hardly any makeup and her fair hair in a ponytail. Now, at nearly thirty, she was a beautiful woman, classy and elegant.

Somehow, though, she'd disappeared during the hubbub after he'd finished "Impossible to Forget" and he'd been surprised—and a little disturbed—by how disappointed he was. As he began his second song, "Trouble is My Middle Name," he told himself to forget her. She'd obviously not wanted to see him. *And you didn't want to see her, either, remember?*

Then halfway through the song, he spied her again. This time she was coming from somewhere off to his left and it was clear she intended to leave because she was heading straight for the door. He made an instant decision not to let that happen. He quickly ended the song after the first chorus and before the notes from the final chord had died away, spoke into the mic, saying, "Eve! Eve Cermak!"

She stopped in midflight and slowly turned as a hush fell over the room. She stared at him.

He grinned. "I thought that was you." He could see

she knew she was trapped. Whether she wanted to talk to him or not, now she would have to.

"Hello, Adam," she finally said. "I—I was trying to sneak out without disturbing anyone."

"Yeah, I saw that."

By now some of the bystanders had begun to murmur, and Adam knew tongues would soon be wagging. "Sorry, y'all," he said, "but Eve and I are old friends from our high school days, and I didn't want her to leave without saying hello to her." He smiled at Eve again. "You don't really have to go, do you? Why don't you stay awhile and talk to me when I'm done here?"

He could see the conflict in her eyes. He knew she wanted to bolt. He also knew she probably wouldn't, because if she did, tongues really *would* wag. After all, this was a small town. And he was the small-town hero, at least for today.

"I—I guess I could stay awhile," she said faintly.

Someone moved over on one of the benches to offer her a seat.

Satisfied, Adam grinned, thanked everyone for their patience and began his third song, this time choosing "My Stars."

And all the while he was singing, he kept his eyes on Eve. And to her credit, she didn't once look away.

Eve knew she was trapped. She couldn't leave now, not until Adam was finished, because if she did, everyone would see her. And they'd wonder, especially after he'd singled her out, why she was leaving. After all, every one of them would probably have given their firstborn to spend time with him, to be able to say they knew Adam Crenshaw. God, even Steve Winthrop, the director of the shelter, and who had been asking her out for months and whom she'd been attempting to let down easy because even though he was a nice guy, he was almost twenty years older than her, and she was not attracted to him, had seen and heard everything Adam had said to her. And Steve was giving her an odd look.

And then there was Alice Fogarty, the nutritionist who volunteered in the shelter's kitchen, and who was a notorious gossip and neighbor of Eve's mother. Alice was standing not two feet away, staring at her, avid curiosity on her face. She'd seen and heard the entire exchange, too. Eve could just imagine what that busybody would have to say about all of this tomorrow, especially what she'd gleefully report to Eve's mother.

Oh, God.

If Eve's mother ever found out the truth—the fallout, the consequences, didn't bear thinking about.

Oh, yes, Eve was definitely trapped. She would have to stand here and smile and act as if she was enjoying the entertainment until the very end. And then she would have to talk to Adam just as if he were merely an old classmate of hers. Could she do it? Whether she could or she couldn't, she would have to. She had no choice.

So she stood there.

And she smiled.

And she pretended to be enjoying herself.

And all the while, inside, she was quaking.

Finally, after what seemed like hours, but was—in reality—only about thirty more minutes, Adam said he would be happy to take a few questions, and let people take more pictures if they wanted to, but then he needed to go.

Hands immediately flew up. Adam chuckled and called on a skinny young man sitting near the front of the room.

"Did you always know you wanted to be in the music business?" the young man asked.

Adam nodded. "Yep. From the moment I held my first guitar when I was twelve years old."

Eve remembered how he'd once told her that guitar had changed his life. How he'd found a crumpled-up, dirty twenty-dollar bill near the sewer at the end of his street and how he'd hidden it and added to it doing every odd job he could find until he had enough money to buy the guitar from a local pawnshop. How he'd even taken it to bed with him because he was afraid one of his brothers would mess with it, maybe even break it, if he didn't.

"Did you always write your own music?" the young man continued.

"Yeah, I did. Of course, the early attempts weren't very good. I thought everything needed to rhyme and you can't imagine the goofy stuff I came up with. I remember one song where I used *dastard* and *bastard* and *mustard*!"

The entire room burst into laughter. Even Eve had to laugh, although her insides were still trembling with nerves.

"I'd love to hear that one," the young man said when the room quieted down.

"Oh, no," Adam said. "I wouldn't do that to anybody. That song was pretty awful."

A middle-aged woman that Eve didn't recognize called out, "We're all proud of you, Adam. One of our own making it big."

"Thank you, ma'am," he said. "I've been lucky."

"It ain't luck, son," an older man Eve knew by the name of Joshua said. "It's pure grit and determination."

"And talent!" said Marcy Winters, the choir director of St. Nicholas Catholic Church, where Eve was a member.

Adam answered a few more questions, allowed a couple dozen more pictures to be taken, then began to pack up his guitar while people milled around him. Finally he managed to extricate himself, and he headed in Eve's direction. Eve knew all eyes in the room were on them as he reached her side and smiled down at her.

"Would you like to go have coffee with me or something?" he asked quietly.

What I want is to run out of here as fast as my legs can carry me and go home and hide. "Sure," she said, hoping she looked calmer than she felt. "Sounds good."

A few minutes later, outside in the balmy night air, she suggested they walk over to Dinah's Diner on the town square.

"Dinah's Diner is a new one on me," Adam said.

"It only opened about three years ago. Dinah Campbell—you may have known her as Dinah Bloom—took over the old Burger Shack space."

"I remember that place."

Eve nodded. She knew he would. Burger Shack had been the hangout of choice for teenagers when they were in school. Not that Adam and Eve had ever gone there. No way they could have kept their relationship secret if they had.

Of course, Adam hadn't been the one who'd wanted to keep it secret. That was all her doing. She hadn't wanted to tell him, but she'd been forced to, that her parents would never permit her to see him.

"Do you always do everything your parents tell you to do?" he'd asked.

It had embarrassed her to admit it, but she'd been honest and said, "Yes, I do."

"Yet you're lying to them now," had been his rejoinder, "so you don't always do what they say, do you?"

She still remembered the way he'd looked at her when he'd said it. Even then, as inexperienced and naive as she was, she'd known it was going to be very hard to ever say no to him.

Dinah's was only about half-full when they got there, but the low buzz when they entered the place told Eve every single person there knew exactly who Adam was and, before long, they'd know who she was, too, if they didn't already.

One of the booths that lined the windows facing the street was empty and Adam suggested they take it. As the waitress—a cute teenager named Liz whom Eve knew from church—approached, he said, "I'm starving, so I'm gonna order food. How 'bout you?"

Eve had only picked at the chicken salad she'd had for dinner. "I could eat a cheeseburger. They're really good here."

"Let's go for it," he said, smiling.

That dimple of his would be her undoing. Or maybe she was already undone. After all, she was here with him, wasn't she?

They both ordered the cheeseburgers and a basket of rosemary fries to share. "Rosemary fries?" he said in mock disbelief.

"Just because we're a small town doesn't mean we're hicks," Eve said, grinning.

"They're really good," the waitress, who was obviously starstruck, said.

Once she was gone, he leaned back and smiled at Eve. "You've grown into a beautiful woman, Eve," he said softly.

Eve knew she was blushing. She could feel the heat warming her cheeks. "Thank you." She ducked her head. "You're not so bad yourself."

He made a face. "Yeah, sexiest man alive. Did you hear?"

"I did."

He shook his head. "What bull."

"I don't think it is."

"Really? You think I'm sexy?" He struck a pose. "I could do that old Rod Stewart song."

But she didn't rise to the bait. Instead, she said quietly, "I always did."

The words seemed to float between them in air that was suddenly charged with emotions struggling to surface. For a long moment, neither of them spoke, then both spoke at the same time.

"Eve, why didn't you—?"

"Adam, I'm sorry I—"

They stopped, and he said, "You go first."

Eve took a deep breath. "I just wanted you to know I'm sorry I never got to say goodbye."

His eyes locked with hers. They were a shade of gray that always made her think of rainy streets. "I wasn't surprised you didn't show up that night."

Because she didn't know what to say to that statement, she said nothing. Out of the corner of her eye, she spied their waitress coming with their food anyway, so it was better to stay quiet, at least for now.

As if he knew they'd neared territory better left alone, he began to eat, and for a while, they didn't talk at all. Then someone fed the jukebox and "Love Me Tender" began to play.

"One of my all-time favorite songs," Adam said between bites.

"Mine, too," Eve said. Their eyes once again met. The expression in his made her heart trip. She couldn't believe he still had the power to make her feel this way. It was almost as if twelve years had gone up in smoke. Or had never been.

Just as Adam opened his mouth to say something, Eve sensed someone standing nearby. She looked up and saw Joe Ferguson, the mayor of Crandall Lake.

"Just thought I'd stop by and say hello," Ferguson said. "I've been hoping I'd have the chance to welcome one of our most famous sons back to town." He stuck out his hand. "Joe Ferguson, mayor of our fair city."

Adam wiped his hand on his napkin and shook Ferguson's. "Nice to meet you."

"I hear you were over at the shelter tonight, entertaining the troops," Ferguson said. His florid face looked even redder under the bright lights of the diner.

"Yes, I stopped by."

"I was hopin' maybe I could persuade you to come to the Rotary Club meetin' on Tuesday, give us a little concert there."

"Um, I'm not sure I can. I'll have to see how my mother's doing," Adam hedged.

Eve couldn't stand Joe Ferguson. He was one of those politicians who'd been in office way too long but seemed impossible to unseat. He had a vastly inflated opinion of himself and seemed oblivious to the fact a lot of people didn't share that view.

"Sure, I understand. Well, you can let me know on Monday. And if Tuesday doesn't work out, we can find another date."

All this time Ferguson had acted as if Eve wasn't there, not that she minded. But Adam noticed, for he said, "I don't know if you've met Eve Cermak—"

"Eve Kelly," Eve corrected. "And Mayor Ferguson and I know each other from church."

"Yeah, of course," Ferguson said. "I see you at St. Nick's all the time."

Now Eve noticed someone else approaching their table. She looked at Adam, telegraphing her wish to leave, and it worked, for he immediately said, "You know, we really need to get going. I'm planning on going back to the hospital tonight and it's getting late."

"Oh, sure. No problem," Ferguson said. He fished in his shirt pocket and pulled out a card. "My cell number is on that. You can call me about Tuesday night either tomorrow or Monday. Try to come, okay? All the guys are wantin' to meet you."

"Is it just me or is he kind of obnoxious?" Adam said after they'd made their escape.

"He's definitely obnoxious," Eve said, laughing. "I couldn't wait to get away from him."

They were outside on the sidewalk now. Adam looked around. "Where's your car?"

"I walked to the shelter."

"Really? Where do you live?"

"Over on Maple Avenue, just off Center Street. It's not far."

"It's far enough. I'll walk you home."

"You don't have to do that."

"Eve, it's nine o'clock. It's dark. I'm not letting you walk by yourself."

"It's perfectly safe. I walk at night all the time. You've been living in the big city too long, Adam. You've forgotten what small-town life is like."

"I don't care. I'm still walking you home."

"But you said you have to go back to the hospital."

"I lied. I just wanted to get away from your esteemed mayor."

"He's not *my* esteemed mayor. I haven't voted for him in either of the past two elections."

"Whatever. I don't have to go to the hospital, and I *am* walking you home."

Because it was obvious nothing she could say was going to change his mind, and she didn't want to argue with him, Eve shrugged and said, "Okay, fine." But down deep, she knew these weren't the only reasons she was letting him have his way.

Whether it was wise or not, she wasn't ready to say goodbye.

Chapter Four

When Adam offered his arm, Eve only hesitated a moment before taking it. It felt good to walk together, especially as he matched his strides to hers. As they walked along, the years melted away, and for those few minutes, being with him felt exactly right.

The soft night air surrounded them, and everywhere there were night sounds: crickets chirping, doves cooing and, in the distance, tires humming along the nearby highway. And somewhere not far away the lilting notes of a violin drifted toward them. Eve could smell the sweet fragrance of night jasmine and roses. It was a perfect night.

It didn't take long to reach her house. For a moment, they stood awkwardly on the sidewalk. Quickly, before she could change her mind, she said, "Would you like to stay and talk awhile?"

He smiled. "I'd like that very much."

So they climbed the steps to the porch, and she invited him to sit on the swing. "I have some freshly made lemonade. Can I tempt you with a glass?"

"Sounds great."

Why had she invited him to stay? she asked herself as she walked indoors. Wouldn't it have been better to simply thank him and say good-night?

But you didn't want to say good-night, did you?

No, she hadn't. She'd finally relaxed enough to enjoy being in his company, and she was curious about him. There were all kinds of things she wanted to ask him, and in the privacy of her porch, with no prying eyes to watch them, she could. She might never again have this opportunity, so she'd taken it.

She put the glasses of lemonade on a small tray and added a plate of peanut-butter cookies, about the only kind she could make that actually turned out well. She'd baked them thinking the twins would be home tonight, and since they weren't, she might as well put them to good use. Especially since, if Mayor Ferguson hadn't interrupted them, she would have recommended the really excellent banana-cream pie at Dinah's.

When she rejoined Adam on the porch, he smiled. "Peanut-butter cookies! I haven't had homemade ones since I was a kid."

"I know. They remind me of being a kid, too." Eve sat next to him on the swing. "So I read that your band is starting a big autumn tour and your first date will be in Austin in September."

"That's the plan."

"I was actually thinking of trying to get tickets."

"Were you? I'll give you passes if you want to come."

"Oh, that would be great. Thank you." She hesitated, then added, "I'm really proud of you, Adam. You've done so well."

"Thanks. There've been some rough patches, but overall, I'm happy with the way things have gone. And what about you? Did you go to college like you planned?"

"Yes, but not exactly the way I'd planned. I could only go part-time because I had the twins, so it took me about six years to finish."

"Twins? I didn't know that."

"Yes, a boy and a girl. Natalie and Nathan." Even saying their names to him caused her heart to flutter alarmingly.

"How old are they?"

"Um, they're eleven."

He looked over at her, and she wondered what he was thinking.

"You married that guy who was always hanging around your family's house, didn't you? That friend of your family's."

"Bill Kelly. Our parents were best friends."

"I always thought he was lookin' to score with you."

Eve had sensed the same thing, even though Bill had never said anything until after Adam was gone. And even then, he probably would have bided his time, thinking she was too young, but she was such a mess and so vulnerable, he had seen his chance and he'd taken it.

"You married him almost right away," Adam said.

"Not right away. It was…about three months later."

She had nothing to feel guilty about. After all, Adam was the one who had left. Adam was the one who had never returned her calls.

"Did you love him?"

"That…that's not a fair question."

"I think it's fair. I loved you, Eve. I thought you loved me. We were going away together. And three months later you marry someone else? Don't you think you owe me an explanation?"

I don't owe you anything.

"You never called me." She couldn't keep the bitterness out of her voice.

"You were the one who didn't show up that night."

"I didn't think you'd go without me!" she cried. "And I did try to call you. I tried several times, but the number just rang and rang. And I didn't know how else to get in touch with you."

He put his now-empty glass down on the little table next to the swing and stared at her. "You tried to call me?"

"Yes."

"Why?"

"I—" She stopped. What could she say? It was too late to say anything.

"Why, Eve? Were you sorry? What?"

"I—I just wanted to talk to you."

"When did you call?"

"What does it matter?" She could feel tears welling. Dammit. She would not cry. She wouldn't!

"It matters 'cause I didn't get any calls."

"Well, I called. Not right away."

"When?" he pressed.

"I don't know exactly!" But she *did* know exactly.

She remembered the day almost to the hour. "It…it was about three or four weeks later."

"That explains it."

"Explains what?"

"I no longer had my cell phone. I ran out of money and had to give up the phone. Couldn't afford it. It was a couple of weeks before I could get another one."

"But the number *rang*!"

"It just sounded as if it was ringing. You were calling a dead line."

"I see." She thought about the misery she'd felt then, when he'd never answered his phone. The heartache and then the panic.

"You never answered my question."

"What question?"

"Were you sorry? Is that why you were calling me?"

Eve sighed deeply. "It really doesn't matter now, Adam." She thought he was going to keep pushing her to answer him, but he didn't. Instead, all the fight seemed to leave him and he slumped back and closed his eyes.

Eve felt tears forming again. Oh, she hated how she cried so easily. *Don't let yourself feel sorry for him. He has a wonderful life, everything he ever dreamed of. And you? You have the twins. Don't forget that.*

After a long moment of quiet, he opened his eyes and said, "Were you happy, Eve?"

"Happy enough, I guess."

"But you didn't stay together."

"No. We divorced four years ago."

"And you have two children."

"Yes."

"Where are they? Don't they live with you?"

"Half the time they do. Bill and I share custody and they're with him until tomorrow night. What about you? You ever think about marriage? Kids?"

"I think about it," he said, "but there's never been anyone I wanted to marry." He didn't say *except you*.

They fell into another awkward silence, and Eve decided it was time to steer the conversation into a less sensitive area. Besides, there were lots of things she was curious about. "Tell me about your mom. How's she doing?"

"She's actually doing great. She'll be moving to rehab on Monday."

"I'm glad. I know you've been worried."

For the next hour or so he told her all about his life: his brothers, his career, his plans for the future. And she told him about her family, her parents—Eve's dad had died a few months after she and Bill divorced—her career, her doubts and her fears. As they talked, he interjected comments, and many times, he made her laugh. Eve realized he'd always had the ability to make her laugh. She missed it.

Finally, she realized how late it was. "It's nearly midnight, Adam," she said. "And I'm the lector at nine o'clock Mass tomorrow. I have to get to bed."

He immediately got up. "I'm sorry. I didn't realize it was so late."

"It's okay. I loved talking to you. It…it's been great seeing you again." She stood, too.

They stood there facing each other, and it seemed like the most natural thing in the world for him to lean forward to kiss her good-night. It was probably meant to be a light touching of lips against lips, and it even began that way, but the moment their lips met, Eve felt a charge all the way down to her toes. She knew he felt it, too, because his hands, which had been placed lightly on her shoulders, tightened, and he pulled her closer, deepening the kiss.

When his tongue slipped into her mouth, she wound her arms around his neck and all the longing and pain and love that had been suppressed and denied for twelve long years burst forth into a desire so intense, Eve couldn't have controlled it even if she'd wanted to.

And she didn't want to. What she wanted was more. What she wanted was for him to never stop kissing her. She forgot where she was, where *they* were. She forgot that anyone passing by could see them against the lit windows. She forgot everything but this man and this moment.

When they finally broke apart, they were both breathing hard.

"Eve…" His voice was ragged.

Oh, my God. "I—I…" *What did I do?* She stared at him. Swallowed. Her heart was still going like a trip-hammer. "I—I have to go in." She reached for door handle.

"Eve, wait."

But she evaded his arm, opened the door and with-out another word, closed it behind her. She was shak-ing, appalled with the way she'd lost control of herself, appalled with the way she'd acted.

What was she going to do now?

And what was *he* going to do?

Would he think the way she'd acted tonight meant they could just pick up where they'd left off twelve years ago?

These questions whirled in her brain as she berated

herself for being so weak. But by the time she heard him leave and realized she'd left their glasses and the empty plate outside and retrieved them, she had calmed down and come to a decision.

It didn't matter *what* he thought or what had happened tonight. From now on, she was going to have to be stronger than she'd ever been, because if Adam was wrong for her all those years ago, if a relationship with him was impossible then, it was unthinkable now.

Eve had a hard time falling asleep. Although she kept telling herself the time she'd spent with Adam that evening meant nothing—would certainly *lead* to nothing—it didn't seem to make any difference. She couldn't stop thinking about him: how he'd looked, what he'd said, what he *hadn't* said, and especially the kiss he'd given her just before leaving. How could such a kiss— starting as nothing more than a feathery touch—have affected her so strongly, and become so passionate so quickly? Even thinking about it brought on butterflies.

That she shouldn't see him again was a given. No matter how she felt about him or he might feel about her, their history alone made seeing him too dangerous. The phrase "playing with fire" was made for this situation, because that was exactly what she would be doing.

She should never have gone to the shelter. The fact she hadn't known he'd be there wasn't an excuse. She'd known he was in town, so she should have avoided any unknown situation. Put her head down and never taken any chance she'd bump into him. It had been stupid to give anyone here any reason to ever connect the two of them. Because if anyone ever put two and two together, ever found out the truth…

Her heart thumped painfully.

The truth.

In her case, it wouldn't set her free. It would only cause heartache and turmoil. For so many people…

Why did I ask him to stay? Why didn't I just thank him for walking me home and say good-night? I knew I shouldn't spend time with him, yet I did it anyway. Oh, God. Nothing has changed. I still can't resist him. All my good sense flies out the window when he's around. Then I do crazy things.

These thoughts and more tumbled over and over in her mind, keeping her awake long into the night. As a result, she only got about four hours of sleep, and even a hot shower and strong cup of coffee wasn't enough to make her feel as fresh as she needed to be the following morning. She tried, though. She put on her favorite sleeveless dress—red linen and a matching red headband—and made sure her makeup was flawless. After all, even a sinking ship wanted to look good going down, she thought wryly as she gave herself one last once-over in the mirror.

Normally, Eve enjoyed serving as a lector at Mass on Sundays. But because of her turbulent night and lack of sleep, she had a hard time concentrating on the readings and knew she wasn't at her best. Still, somehow she got through the service without making any glaring mistakes. She was doubly glad, because she knew her mother had attended the service. She'd seen Anna going to communion. So she wasn't surprised to spy her mother standing at the back of the church after

Mass. She cringed, though, when she saw the woman standing next to her.

Alice Fogarty's eyes were alight as Eve approached the two women, and Eve knew she was in for a grilling about Adam. Sure enough, the first words out of Alice's mouth were, "Well, here's your dark-horse daughter now, Anna. I can't believe she never told you she was such good friends with Adam Crenshaw!"

Eve's heart sank. It was going to be even worse than she'd imagined. Pasting a smile on her face, she said levelly, "I'd hardly call us good friends, Alice." Turning her gaze to her mother, she leaned in for a hug. "We were classmates, Mom," she said as they drew apart.

"Well, I didn't see him singling out any *other* classmates last night," Alice said, "and if I'm not mistaken, Todd Winsen was also in your class."

Damn the woman. Was there anything she *didn't* know about the people in Crandall Lake? Todd Winsen, who was also a volunteer at the shelter and had been there the night before, had indeed been a classmate.

"Well, wasn't he?" Alice pressed as the three women headed to the activity center, where coffee and doughnuts were served after each Mass. Eve hadn't planned to stay, but she knew there was no polite way she could avoid it now, especially since she normally *did* visit with her mother when they ended up at the same Mass.

"Yes, he was," Eve said. Although she would never wish Alice any real harm, maybe the woman could trip and sprain an ankle or something. Anything to get her mind off Adam Crenshaw and on to something else.

"So c'mon, tell us. What did he have to say? Is his mother okay? How long is he gonna stay in Crandall Lake?"

During all these questions, Eve's mother had been suspiciously quiet, and Eve wondered what she was thinking. Knowing her mother and how she valued her privacy, she knew she wouldn't be adding any fodder to Alice's penchant for gossip, but she must have a lot of questions of her own, and Eve was sure once they were alone, she would give voice to them. Because it *was* odd that over the years Eve had never once mentioned Adam. If they really had been "old friends" as he had claimed, it would have been natural to talk about him.

"He said his mother is doing well and will be moved to rehab tomorrow," Eve finally said, knowing she had to give Alice some answers if she ever wanted the woman to move on to another subject.

"That's good," Eve's mother finally said. Her eyes were thoughtful as they met Eve's. "From what I know of the family, she's had a rough time."

"Maybe that was true early on, before her son became famous," Alice declared, just as if she had firsthand knowledge of the Crenshaws. "Her husband was a drunk—we all know that. But I'm sure her sons have taken good care of her ever since. She probably has it a lot easier than either you *or* me, Anna. After all, she now lives in Royal Oaks, and we sure don't!"

To Eve's mother's credit, she gave Alice a disparaging look. "Even though we're both widows, neither of us has a hard life, Alice. In fact, we should both count our blessings every day."

Eve couldn't help smiling. That was her mother. *Count your blessings. Don't borrow trouble. Put a good face on it.* Anna Cermak loved those old truisms. Had always lived by them. Of course, Eve herself had been thinking the same thing last night when she'd gone to the shelter, hadn't she? Another of Anna's truisms popped into her mind: the apple doesn't fall far from the tree. Eve almost laughed, and if she hadn't been so uncomfortable with the subject, she might have.

"For heaven's sake, Anna," Alice said, "of course I know that. But still…Lucy Crenshaw could have anything she wanted now. I mean, her son must make millions!" Turning back to Eve, she said, "Is he going to stay here in Crandall Lake for a while?"

"I have no idea. He didn't discuss his plans."

"Well, what *did* he discuss?"

Since Eve couldn't say it was none of Alice's business, she said, "Not much, Alice. We didn't talk long. I, um…had to get home."

"You must have talked about *something*," Alice insisted. "I heard you went to Dinah's."

Eve mentally sighed. She'd hoped to pretend the evening had ended soon after they'd left the shelter, but once again, the small-town grapevine had been hard at work. "Yes. He was hungry."

"So what'd he talk about?" Alice pressed.

Just as Eve was trying to figure out how best to answer, she saw Joe Ferguson walking their way. Not again! She wasn't sure she had the energy to deal with the mayor again right now, especially not in front of Alice. Oh, why hadn't Eve pretended not to be feeling well and escaped the whole coffee-and-doughnuts thing entirely this morning? But maybe it wasn't too late. Standing, she turned to her mother and said, "Mom, I'm really not feeling great and I have to write—"

"Well, lookee here," Ferguson boomed as he reached their table. "If it isn't three of the best-looking women in Crandall Lake. How are y'all doing this fine summer morning, ladies?"

Eve's mother turned and smiled. Alice Fogarty looked less charmed as her eyes met Eve's. Eve took a deep breath, forced another smile and remained standing. "Good morning, Joe. I was just leaving." Turning back to her mother, she added, "I'll call you later, Mom, okay? I really do have to go. I still have to write my blog and the twins will be home later."

"Before you go," Ferguson said, "I was wondering— did you have a chance to talk to Adam about coming to the Rotary meetin' on Tuesday?"

"I'm sorry, Joe. We didn't discuss it." Slinging her purse over her shoulder, she waved goodbye and determinedly strode off without waiting for anyone to say anything else.

As she walked from the activity center to the main church parking lot she berated herself again for ever going to the shelter yesterday. If only she hadn't seen Adam. If only she hadn't been forced to talk to him in front of all those people. If only she hadn't suggested going to Dinah's Diner.

But she had. And she did. And no amount of wishing otherwise would change that. As a result, she knew she had a lot more questioning in store for her, from lots of people.

But mostly from her mother.

And she'd better be certain she had her answers ready.

Adam didn't get to the hospital until early afternoon on Sunday. His mother was napping when he walked in, the remains of her lunch still on her tray table. Her room was filled with the fragrance of flowers, most of them from his friends and colleagues in the music business. His gaze lingered on the large and expensive bouquet sent by Bethany. He didn't have to look at the accompanying card to know what it said:

Praying for a speedy recovery for you. Love from Bethany

He shook his head. It was past time to tell Bethany how he felt. It wasn't fair to keep her thinking their relationship was ever going to go any further. He was turning over options of when and what to say when his phone buzzed. Almost as if he'd conjured her with his thoughts, the incoming text was from Bethany.

Call me when you get a min. Important!!!

This was the third text she'd sent in the past hour. He decided since his mother was still sleeping, he would go out to the waiting area and place the call. Otherwise, Bethany would just keep texting, and sooner or later, she'd get tired of doing that and start calling herself.

She answered on the first ring.

"I was beginning to think you were purposely ignoring me," she said.

"I was in the shower when you first texted, driving when you texted again and in my mother's hospital room this time."

"Why didn't you call me after you got out of the shower?"

Adam stifled a sigh. "I'm calling you now. What's up?"

"What's up is you've been gone more than a week! And *Rolling Stone* waits for no man."

Now Adam really did sigh. "Just cancel the interview, okay?"

"Okay? No, it's not okay. You can't cancel *Rolling Stone*. Not if you care about your career."

"Look, even they must understand that if a man's mother has a heart attack, that's a little bit more important than an interview."

"Your mom is fine now, Adam. Don't pretend she isn't."

"She's doing better, yes. But she's not completely out of the woods."

"Austin told me she's moving to rehab tomorrow. That her prognosis is very positive."

"When did you talk to Austin?"

"Last night."

Adam frowned. Had Austin called her? Or vice versa?

"I tried calling you, and when you didn't pick up, I called him. I mean, I need to be kept in the loop! At least Austin understands that."

"I was planning to call you."

"When? Next week? Next month?"

"You know, Bethany, you don't own me. Just because—"

"When are you coming home?" she said, interrupting him.

Although he wanted to lash out at her, Adam knew it was best to count to ten. This was not the time or the place for their overdue conversation. So he kept his voice even. "I don't know yet. I want to see how my mother does in rehab. And then we have to find a good housekeeper/caretaker for her. None of us want her living on her own any longer." He thought about saying he actually hoped to persuade his mother to come back to Nashville with him, then thought better of it.

For a long moment, all he heard was Bethany breathing, and he knew she was probably counting to ten herself. The fair part of him acknowledged she had a right to be angry. When she finally spoke again, her voice was even, as well. "How about if I have the reporter from *Rolling Stone* come to Crandall Lake to see you?"

"No. Have him...or her...call me instead. We'll set something up."

"But—"

"I don't want anyone coming here. This is my home. It has nothing to do with my career." The last thing he wanted was some reporter poking around in his past.

"That's the most naive thing I've ever heard you say," Bethany said. "Everything in your life has to do with your career!"

"That's a sad commentary on celebrity today," he muttered.

"It may be sad, but that doesn't make it any less true."

Adam sighed. He could feel another headache coming on. Bethany seemed to have that effect on him more and more lately. "Just have him call me. We'll work it out. Now I really have to go. We'll talk tomorrow, after I get my mother settled."

He knew, as he disconnected the call, that he'd only postponed the inevitable. He couldn't help thinking he should have listened to Austin six months ago, when he and Bethany had first started dating. Austin had warned him mixing business with his personal life wasn't a good idea, but Adam hadn't paid attention. His brother had been right. Breaking it off with a girl-friend was hard enough. Breaking it off with a girl-friend who was also your publicist was a nightmare. Would he have to get rid of Bethany altogether? Or could they continue to work together? He guessed he wouldn't know until they actually talked.

And the sooner, the better.

Chapter Five

Bill brought the twins home at six o'clock. "Perfect timing," Eve told him. "Just finished writing my blog and sending it off."

Turning to the children, she said, "Did you guys have fun?"

"Yes, yes," they chimed together.

"It was a great weekend," Bill said. "What's on the agenda for them this week?"

Although Eve disliked the proprietary way he seemed to think he had any say in how she handled her weeks of custody, she understood why he'd asked the question, because school was now officially over for the summer, and she was a working mother. "I've enrolled them in the Y's day camp this week."

"Cool!" Natalie said, her gray eyes alight with excitement.

Nathan dimpled, his grin wide and just as happy as his sister's. "Outstanding!" he said. *Outstanding* was his current favorite adjective.

In that moment, standing there with the father they'd loved and adored from the moment they were born, Eve's heart clutched. They were such terrific kids, and she loved them so much.

"Sounds good," Bill said. "Then, I'll see you guys Friday night."

"No," Eve said, shaking her head. "They'll be with me next weekend. You had this weekend, remember?"

"But it's Madison's birthday party next Saturday," Bill said. Madison was his sister Sheila's daughter. The family lived in Houston.

"Mom, we can't miss Madison's party!" Natalie said. "We're going roller-skating."

"And we're all going to Chuck E. Cheese's after the skating!" Nathan said.

"And then that night, the girls are having a sleepover," Natalie said.

"It's gonna be outstanding," Nathan said.

Eve wanted to cry foul, but she knew, looking at the disappointment on her kids' faces, that she'd lost before she'd lobbed the first ball. She sighed, looked at Bill. "I forgot."

"I'm sorry." He took her hand, his blue eyes filled with genuine empathy.

That was the thing about Bill. He really did understand how she felt because he would have felt the same way. Why did he have to be so nice? And so fair? Why couldn't he be an SOB so she could hate him? But of course, if he'd been an SOB she'd never have married him. And he'd never have offered. It was precisely because of the kind of man he was that he *had* offered. And that he'd never, not once, thrown the circumstances of that offer into her face—not even when they'd divorced.

"I know," she said. "It's okay. They'll be ready Friday night. What time?"

"Five?"

"All right."

The kids gave Bill a hug and kiss, said their goodbyes, and he turned to leave, but not before saying, "Eve? Walk me out?"

She knew he wanted to talk and didn't want the kids to hear. What now? she wondered.

He waited till they'd reached his SUV before saying, "I heard Adam Crenshaw is in town."

She stiffened. "Yes."

"I also heard about what happened at the shelter last night."

Eve guessed she shouldn't be surprised. Bill had lived in Crandall Lake all his life. Most of his clients lived here, too. Someone who knew him was bound to have told him. She should have expected that.

"I didn't know he would be there when I went," she said, trying not to sound defensive.

Bill's eyes were thoughtful as they studied hers.

She sighed. "Bill, I promise you, he has no idea…"

Bill nodded. "I only wanted to remind you that we have a deal. He's never to know."

"I know that. I won't break my promise."

"I'm their father."

"Yes, you are."

For a long moment, they just stared at each other, each remembering that long-ago promise.

"How long is he staying here?" Bill finally asked.

"I don't know. Until his mother is back home and settled, I guess."

"Are you planning to see him again?"

"No. I—I think it's best if I don't." *Oh, God. If Bill knew everything that happened last night...*

"Yes. So do I." He hesitated, then added, "Look, Eve, I know this is hard. I know you probably want to tell him. But you can't—"

"I *don't* want to tell him! That's the *last* thing I want."

He studied her for another long moment, then nodded again. "Good. We're both on the same page, then."

As Eve watched her ex drive off, she knew she had no reason to resent Bill for asking about Adam or for reminding her of their long-ago agreement, and yet, down deep, she did.

Because even though they were divorced, and she was supposedly a free woman, she would never have full control over her life. Her long-ago decision would always hang over her head and impact her future.

But the twins were secure and happy, and that was the most important thing. She must never forget that.

The rest of the evening was spent fixing dinner, hearing all about the kids' weekend and watching a couple of television shows together. Because there was no school tomorrow, Eve let the twins stay up until ten, but finally they were settled into bed, she'd heard their prayers and had kissed them good-night.

Slowly, she walked out to the front porch and sat on the swing. As she gazed out at the moonlight-drenched yard, her thoughts alternated between Adam and the way he still made her feel, and how she had to avoid him from now on, then they'd veer toward Bill and the children. She thought about all the years since the twins had been born. And she finally let her mind drift back to the day that had been hovering at the back of her mind ever since Adam had returned to Crandall Lake.

The day she had tried never to think about, but couldn't seem to forget. The day everything had changed.

July, twelve years earlier...

He had been gone from Crandall Lake for five weeks. Five weeks in which she'd cried every night and second-guessed herself every day. Down deep, Eve knew she'd done the right thing. All she had to do was look at her parents and see how happy they were, how proud as they prepared for her to enter college, to know she'd had no other choice.

And yet...

Adam's face haunted her.

What had he thought when she hadn't shown up? Was he as lonely and miserable as she was? Or had he been angry?

For days afterward, she'd thought he would call her. Even though she didn't have a cell phone, he could have called. He'd done it before. Yes, there was always a chance her father would answer, but her father was gone during the day, during the week. No, the reason Adam hadn't called was because he was probably disgusted with her. He probably thought she didn't love him enough. He'd been let down by the people who supposedly cared about him all of his life, so it wouldn't have surprised him to be let down again.

She wanted to tell him how much she loved him, how much she'd wanted to go away with him. It killed her not to tell him. Not to explain. But what good would explaining do anyway? It wouldn't change anything. She still couldn't leave Crandall Lake.

She thought about him so much she made herself sick. She couldn't eat. Couldn't sleep. She was so miserable, she even stopped having her period.

And then, when he'd been gone five weeks and three days, it happened. She'd just gotten out of the shower and was drying herself off when she winced. Her breasts hurt. Confused, she felt them, and yes, they were tender, and they hurt.

She stared at them. Swallowed. As the enormity of her thought expanded, her heart began to thud.

She abruptly sat on the edge of the tub.

Was it possible?

Was she pregnant?

She thought back to the night in May when she had given herself to Adam. Once. Just once. She counted back. Almost nine weeks ago.

She began to shake. *Hail Mary, full of grace, our Lord is with Thee.* The words of the prayer were a whisper, a plea, a denial. It couldn't be true. It couldn't!

Please, God. Please, Holy Mother. Please, please, please...

But no amount of praying changed anything. For three more days, Eve moved through the hours like a zombie. She couldn't seem to think. Couldn't do anything but pray. Finally, though, she knew she had to call Adam. She waited until her mother had gone grocery shopping and placed the call. The number rang and rang and rang, but he never answered. Twice more, over the next day, she called. And twice more, there was no answer at all. Not even voice mail.

Her mother kept asking her what was wrong. Eve kept lying and saying nothing. But sooner or later, she would have to tell her parents. And then what? She would break their hearts.

Even years later, she wasn't sure what she'd have done if Bill hadn't shown up at their house the following afternoon and asked Eve's mother if he could take Eve out for a ride.

"I have to drive over to San Marcos to see a client, and I thought Eve might want to visit the campus. You know, check out her dorm."

Anna had been delighted. Ellen Ruth Kelly, Bill's mother, was Anna's best friend, and the two families had been close for what seemed like forever. The Kellys were Eve's godparents, and her parents were Bill's. Bill was almost like a son.

So Eve, glad to escape her mother's scrutiny, went with Bill. But seeing the campus, knowing she probably wouldn't be going to college that fall, had been her downfall. She'd tried to hide her unhappiness, but Bill knew her too well.

"What's wrong, Eve?" he asked, putting his arm around her shoulder.

She shook her head. What could she say?

"C'mon. You can tell me."

His gentleness was her undoing. She began to cry, her entire body shaking. Alarmed, he guided her to a shady bench and they sat. He kept his arm around her, and she allowed the comfort it afforded. The whole story came tumbling out. When she finished, she felt drained. "I don't know what to do," she said, closing her eyes. She waited for his censure.

"I do," he said.

Her eyes opened and she stared at him.

"Marry me," he said. "Marry me and let me be your baby's father."

"But, Bill, how—?"

"I love you, Eve. I've always loved you. You know that, right?"

She shook her head.

"You must have known. Why do you think I've kept coming by? Wanting to see you?"

"We…we're friends," she stammered. "Our families…"

"I've loved you for years. I was just waiting until you got older."

"You…you *love* me?"

"I do. And I want to marry you. I want to be the father of your children."

When she would have protested, he put his hand over her mouth.

"Don't say no. This is the perfect solution. The boy, the baby's father, he's gone, right?"

"Y-yes, he's gone," she whispered. She had not told him Adam's name or where Adam had gone, but she knew she would have to.

"And he didn't return your phone calls."

"No."

"Well, then…this is the perfect solution. It's the perfect time, too. I'm out of college now and have a good job. I can take care of you. We'll get married right away. Our baby will come a little early, but our parents won't care. They've wanted us to get together for years. They'll be happy."

"I—I don't know…"

"Of course you do. This is meant to be."

It didn't take long for Eve to see Bill was right. Marrying him *was* the perfect solution.

A little less than seven months later, their twins were born. Nathan James and Natalie Jean Kelly. Bill's name was on the birth certificate.

He was their father.

And always would be.

"Eve, I know you've been worried about the layoffs." Joan Wallace, the owner of the *Crandall Lake Courier*, leaned back in her chair.

"We all have," Eve said. It was Monday morning, and Eve had just arrived at the offices of the paper, only to be immediately called into her boss's office.

"Well, I won't keep you in suspense any longer," Joan said. "You're not in any danger of being laid off."

Relief coursed through Eve.

"However, there are going to be some changes."

That didn't surprise Eve. As the public increasingly relied on the internet for their news, the *Courier* had steadily been losing money. Fewer readers meant less advertising revenue. Change was inevitable.

"We're letting Penny go," Joan continued, "so you'll not only be covering city news, you'll be taking over lifestyle and entertainment, too."

Eve's heart sank. Her workload would double. And not only that, it was going to double at the worst possible time of year—the beginning of summer—when she wanted to spend less time at work, not more. Her mind raced. What would she do about the twins? They were too old for day care and not old enough to be on their own.

They can always stay at Bill's for the summer.

She wiped the unwelcome thought away. Yes, that was always an option, but she would only resort to that solution if she became desperate. Maybe her mother would be willing to keep them during the days Eve couldn't work at home.

Joan looked at her thoughtfully. "That means you'll have to spend more time here and out in public and less time working from home."

"I know."

"Will that be a problem?"

"I'll make sure it isn't." Eve couldn't afford to let anything be a problem if it meant keeping her job and her paycheck. Although Bill was generous with money and never questioned what she did with his child-support payments, Eve needed to work. The money she earned wasn't an option; it was a necessity.

"One very good thing—your blog is really taking off." Joan smiled. "I'm tremendously pleased at the numbers we're seeing."

Eve returned the smile. She was pleased, too. A year ago, when Joan had first approached her about blogging, Eve had thought she would do something geared to working mothers. But after doing some research, she'd seen that there were tons of blogs on that subject, but no one seemed to be blogging about small-town life. And so "The Front Porch" was born. Twice a week Eve wrote about small-town living as seen from her front porch. And for some reason, the blog had found an audience. She had lots of steady readers, more and more all the time. Some had suggested she even turn past blogs into a book, and she'd been seriously considering it.

"Does Penny know she's being let go?" Eve asked after a moment.

"I'm calling her in next," Joan said. "I hate doing this, but I don't have a choice."

"I know."

"So later, after I talk to her, maybe you can go over things with her. Find out if there's anything hanging fire that you'll need to complete."

Eve nodded, dreading the meeting with Penny, who was a friend, and who was bound to be upset. She needed her paycheck, too. "Okay."

"And one more thing before you go… I know Penny was planning to try to get an interview with Adam Crenshaw while he's in town. Since according to the grapevine, you seem to know him, that'll be your assignment now."

Eve hoped her expression didn't reveal the instant turmoil Joan's words had caused. She'd promised Bill she would not see Adam again. And although she resented having to do so, she knew, given her circumstances, not seeing him again was her wisest course.

What was she going to do now?

The rest of the morning turned out to be even more stressful than her interview with Joan had been. Penny wasn't the only staffer to get bad news that day. The classified-advertising manager's job was cut and her duties were given to the display-advertising manager. Neither woman was happy. In addition, the circulation manager's hours were cut to half time and the front desk person was given her walking papers, which meant her duties would now be covered by the office manager/bookkeeper, who already had a full load.

Eve wished she could avoid seeing the crestfallen faces, but she couldn't leave before talking with Penny. The talk did not go well. Penny was so close to tears, she had a hard time discussing the status of various stories in progress. But at least she didn't blame Eve.

"Don't feel bad," she finally said. "You've been here longer than anyone. I'm not surprised she's keeping you. Plus, there's your blog. It—it's going so well… I'm…I'm glad for you."

But no matter what Penny said, Eve *did* feel bad. The women at the paper were like one big family, always had been. They celebrated every victory with a covered dish get-together, and every defeat with hugs and support. Now everything would change. But at least Joan hadn't sold the paper. Eve knew her boss had had offers. Good ones, too. But the paper was Joan's baby. She'd started it as a weekly and it had grown to a daily within five years. Joan was as proud of the *Courier* as she was of her two children. Eve knew it was really hard for her to do what she'd had to do today.

Finally, at three o'clock, Eve made her escape. She needed to stop by City Hall and check the calendar, see if there was anything going on this week that she'd need to cover, then she had to pick up the twins at four o'clock. And tonight, after they were settled, she had to try to figure out what she was going to do about the rest of the summer.

She purposely didn't think about Adam and the interview Joan wanted her to get. Like Scarlett O'Hara, she would shelve the problem of Adam until tomorrow.

* * *

The *Rolling Stone* reporter, Ross Edwards, called Adam Monday afternoon. "I could come there," he offered when Adam tried to stall him.

"I'd prefer to wait until I'm back home," Adam said.

"When will that be?"

"Possibly next week."

"Okay, not a problem," Edwards said. "I'll call you on Friday and we'll set a date."

Adam wasn't sure he *would* be back in Nashville next week—he was actually thinking about going straight out to LA where he had his second home—but he'd deal with that question when the time came. For now, he just wanted to focus on writing new music and figuring out his mother's future.

They got Lucy moved to rehab late that afternoon, and Adam and his brothers met with her doctor, who assured them she would probably be going home by the end of the week. "As soon as she's settled into her new routine and used to the change in her diet," the doctor clarified. Adam made a mental note to talk to both Austin and Aaron about his idea of moving her to Nashville in the near future.

Because Lucy was tired and fell asleep shortly after having her evening meal, Adam left for his hotel by six o'clock. Austin had suggested the three brothers have dinner together, but Adam had begged off, saying he needed to work. Yet when he got to his room, he didn't feel like working, nor did he feel like ordering room service. He paced around for a few minutes and tried to decide what he *did* feel like doing.

You want to call Eve. You want to see her again.

He knew there was probably no point in calling her.

From the way she'd acted after they'd kissed the night before, he knew she probably regretted it and didn't want to see him again. Hell, he'd known it last night. But what he knew and what he wanted were two different things. And Adam was used to getting what he wanted.

He called her home number, which was listed, because he'd neglected to get her cell number.

She answered on the second ring. Just the sound of her voice made him want her. "Hello, Eve. It's Adam."

"Hello, Adam."

"I wanted to thank you for last night. It was great seeing you." He would not mention the kiss unless she did.

"I enjoyed it, too."

Okay, so she's going to play it cool and pretend nothing happened. "I was hoping we could do it again. Maybe have dinner sometime this week?"

"That would be difficult. I have the children this week."

"Well, how about this? Instead of going out, I'll bring over a couple of pizzas. I'd like to meet your kids."

"I'm sorry. They're doing Y camp this week and they came home tired and cranky. They'd just get too overexcited if you were to come."

Adam's celebrity was a problem at times, but that wasn't why Eve was putting him off. "How about this—"

"I was going to call you, though," she said, interrupting. "I, um, wondered if you'd let me interview you for the paper."

"Interview me?"

"Yes, um, my boss heard about last night...you know...at the shelter...so she asked me to interview you...since I, uh, know you."

If this was the only way he was going to get to see Eve again, Adam would take it. "Okay. Sure. I'll be glad to give you an interview. When did you want to do it?"

"How about tomorrow afternoon?"

"Why don't we just meet for lunch tomorrow?"

She didn't answer immediately and Adam figured she was searching for a way to avoid lunch. Did she not want to be seen in public with him again? Was that part of her reluctance? "Lunch is the best time for me," he said more firmly. He sensed rather than heard her sigh.

"Well, okay," she said. "Um, where?"

"Why don't you come here, to the Crandall Lake Inn? The food's great and it's quiet. Let's say about twelve thirty?"

She only hesitated a few seconds. "Okay. That sounds good. Thanks, Adam."

"Before you hang up, how about giving me your cell number? Just in case..."

After disconnecting the call, Adam smiled. Knowing he would see Eve again tomorrow, he might even be able to get some work done now. He decided ordering a pizza was a good idea, even if he'd be eating it alone. And tomorrow, when he saw Eve, he'd deal with whatever doubts she had, because no matter what she thought, he wasn't ready to let her disappear from his life again.

Chapter Six

On Tuesday morning, Eve worked from home. She'd just finished getting ready to meet Adam for the lunch interview when her cell rang, and she saw it was Olivia. "Hey, what's up?" she said, answering. Olivia rarely called during working hours.

"I just had to vent to somebody," Olivia said.

Eve knew what was coming.

"Vivienne's at it again." Vivienne Britton was Olivia's mother-in-law, and the two women were not fans of one another.

"What's she done now?" Eve glanced at her watch. She still had twenty minutes before she had to leave for the inn.

"She caused a scene at the day care center. Jessie just called me to tell me."

Jessie was the director of the small day care facility where Olivia left Thea while she was working.

"What was she even doing there?"

"That's a good question! She just showed up. Said she was taking Thea to San Marcos for the day. When Jessie said I hadn't given them written permission and she'd have to call me first, Vivienne blew her stack. You know how she is. She thinks when she says 'jump,' people should jump."

"So what happened?"

"She took Thea anyway. Dared Jessie to try to stop her. The woman is impossible, Eve."

Eve sighed. "I know."

"I should call the police. I should have her arrested."

"Olivia…"

"Oh, I know I can't do that. But I *should*! She has no right to act this way. If Mark were alive…"

Eve could hear the tears threatening. "Hon, calm down. I don't blame you for being upset, but she *is* Thea's grandmother and she wields an awful lot of influence in this town. I doubt the police would have done anything even if you had called them."

"I hate her," Olivia said.

"I know." Eve couldn't stand the woman, either, because Olivia was a good mother yet Vivienne gave her no respect. In fact, she seemed to delight in causing Olivia problems. You'd think she'd worship the ground Olivia walked on. After all, Olivia had given Vivienne her only grandchild so far.

"I'm sorry," Olivia said after a few seconds. "I know you're busy. I shouldn't have bothered you."

"You didn't *bother* me. But I do have to go now. I have an appointment."

"Okay."

"Call me tonight. We can talk more. I want to tell

you about everything that happened at the paper yesterday anyway."

Eve thought about her cousin and her situation as
she drove to meet Adam, and once again thanked the
Lord that she'd had such a wonderful mother-in-law in
Ellen Ruth Kelly. If anything, she had bent over back-
ward to be good to Eve. She'd once laughingly told Bill
in Eve's presence that if he and Eve were ever to split
up—which of course, she knew would never happen!—
she was keeping Eve. Ellen Ruth had died two years
ago from cancer, and not a day went by that Eve didn't
think of her and miss her. She often wondered how
Missy felt about their convoluted relationships.

Olivia's problems and everything else faded from
Eve's mind as she drove her Prius into the wide, curv-
ing driveway of the inn and surrendered her keys to the
valet parking attendant. She'd dressed carefully for today's interview in a lemon-yellow dress and matching
low-heeled pumps. Today, since she was representing
the paper, she'd put her long hair into a neat up twist.
She knew she looked good as she entered the marble-
floored lobby. Her foolish heart skipped when she saw
Adam sitting there waiting for her.

He stood as she approached. Dear heaven, he was
gorgeous! Today he wore casual gray linen pants with
an open-necked white shirt, and he'd tied his shining
hair back from his face. When he smiled, his dimple, so
like Nathan's, and his eyes, so like Natalie's, reminded
her of everything she stood to lose if she wasn't careful.

"You look beautiful," he said, smiling into her eyes.

"Thank you." She told herself to calm down. But
her heart refused to listen.

"Our table's ready for us." Her took her elbow and guided her toward the dining room.

Clutching her purse, telling herself she was a professional reporter and that she could handle anything, Eve allowed herself to be led.

The dining room was only about one-third full. The maître d' showed them to a table by the windows, with a view of the river. The grounds sported jewel-bright flower beds and leafy oak trees, with the sparkling ribbon of water beyond. A couple of fat squirrels chased each other up the trunk of the nearest tree, and Eve couldn't help smiling as she watched them.

"It's a great view, isn't it?" Adam said as they were seated.

"Yes. Crandall Lake may be small, but it's got just about everything," Eve said.

"So you've never been sorry you stayed here."

Eve's eyes met his. "No. Never." *What a liar you are. You're sorry for just about everything.*

He held her gaze steadily. "So why *did* you call me twelve years ago, then?"

Eve sighed. He wasn't going to let go of that question. "I—I wanted to see if you were okay. I wanted to tell you I was sorry."

"You just said you weren't sorry you stayed here."

"But I *was* sorry I'd hurt you."

His face closed up a bit at her words, and she knew she was right. She *had* hurt him. And she finally had a chance to apologize.

She leaned forward, speaking softly. "I was hurt, too, Adam. Even though I couldn't go with you, I cried every day for weeks after you left."

"Why *couldn't* you go?"

"You know why. I told you. My parents… It would have destroyed them. I just…I couldn't do that to them." Oh, God. Why were they talking about this now? Here? Where they had no privacy? This was supposed to be an interview. A business interview. She was supposed to be working. She looked around the room, relieved to see there was no one there she knew personally. Her gaze met Adam's again. "I'm sorry."

Just then, sparing her from further conversation, their waiter approached with water and a basket of warm rolls and herb butter. Eve hurriedly looked at the luncheon menu and made a quick decision to order the lobster bisque. Adam ordered the shrimp étouffée, and the waiter left.

"Shall we begin the interview?" Eve asked once he was gone.

"Why don't we wait till after we eat?" In the sunlit dining room, Adam's eyes looked darker than normal.

Eve wanted to disagree, but decided maybe it was better to concede this point. There was enough tension between them as it was.

So for the next hour, while they ate, they only talked casually about the things he'd been doing since coming home, and she filled him in on the changes at the paper and what they would mean to her future. Neither wanted coffee or dessert, and once Adam had signed for the bill, he suggested they conduct the interview upstairs, in his suite.

"I don't think that's a good idea," Eve said.

"I'm not going to try to seduce you, Eve."

Eve knew she was blushing. "I didn't think you would, but it's still not very professional to go to your room."

"Suite," he corrected. "I'll keep the door to the bedroom closed. I promise."

She sighed. She knew she was going to lose this argument. "Okay, fine." Picking up her purse, she stood.

Eve looked around as they entered the lobby and waited by the elevators. Again, she saw no one she knew. Thank God, she thought. The last thing she needed was for someone to tell her mother or Bill that she'd been seen going up to Adam's room. Actually, she was kind of surprised that no one even seemed interested in the fact that Adam was there. She said as much as they entered the elevator.

"That's one of the things I really like about this place," he said. "No one has bothered me. It's a nice change."

When they reached his suite, she was relieved to see it really was a full-fledged suite with a separate living area filled with comfortable chairs and a sofa. There was even a small dining table with four chairs. She suggested they sit there so she could turn her small recorder on and keep it on the table between them as they talked.

He agreed readily, asked if she'd like anything to drink, and when she said no, sat down kitty-corner from her. Once the recorder was switched on, she asked him to tell her about his first weeks in Nashville.

"They were rough," he admitted. "I ran out of money pretty fast. Like I told you before, I even had to pitch my phone 'cause I couldn't afford it. Just got one of those disposables that were cheaper so I could keep calling producers and they'd have a way of contacting me."

He described how he'd rented the cheapest possible room at a boardinghouse, how he'd made dozens of demos and how just as he was about to give up and try to find a job as a waiter or something, one of the producers he'd contacted called him and signed him.

"I owe everything to Duke," he said. "He's still one of my best friends."

"He recognized your talent," Eve said.

They went on to talk about his first record and how it had shot to the top of *Billboard*'s country charts, then surprised everyone by crossing over to the pop charts when DJs around the country began giving it airtime on pop stations.

"That was a big deal, wasn't it?" Eve asked.

"Yeah. I had no idea. It's a good thing I had Duke, because I was a babe in the woods. People could've taken big advantage of me if not for him. I owe him a lot."

"I'm sure he's made a lot of money off you."

"Doesn't matter. I don't forget my friends, people who're straight and loyal."

Eve nodded. "So what's next? There's a rumor that you've been asked to judge one of the reality singing shows."

Adam gave her a self-deprecating grin. "Yeah, and my agent's hot to trot. Thinks I should do it. I don't know. That kind of thing doesn't really interest me. I'd rather just spend that time writing more music."

Eve smiled. She could've predicted that would be his answer. "How about if I take a couple of pictures? I know my boss will want at least one to accompany the article."

When he agreed, she turned off the recorder, then got out her phone and with its camera, took several candid shots. Once that was done, she said, "I forgot to ask. How does it feel to be home again after all these years?"

"You know how it feels," he said, meeting her eyes.

"No, I don't."

"It feels surreal." When she frowned, he quickly said, "But that's off-the-record. Say it feels good. I like seeing everyone and like seeing that Crandall Lake is still as nice as it always was. Say I'm happy to be here for my mother and I like seeing old friends again. Say I'm looking forward to visiting more often in the future."

"Do you really feel that way? Are you planning on coming back more often?"

"I don't know. Depends."

"On what?"

His eyes pinned hers. "On you."

"On me?" Eve said faintly.

"I've never forgotten you, Eve," he said softly. "That kiss last night, it wasn't an impulse. I wanted to kiss you from the minute I saw you at the shelter. My big hit, 'Impossible to Forget'... I wrote that song because of you."

Eve swallowed. She wanted to look away, but she couldn't. Even when he reached for her hand, her gaze remained glued to his. When he gently pulled her toward him, her stupid heart began to race, and even though her brain screamed, *Danger! Danger! No! Stop! Don't do it!* she didn't resist when he drew her into his arms.

"I want you, Eve."

She closed her eyes as his lips grazed her cheek, and drifted down to her neck.

"I've always wanted you," he whispered.

Every nerve ending in her body seemed to be alive with sensation. And when he raised his head to capture her mouth, she moaned, and instead of stopping him, she kissed him back as if her very life depended upon it.

The kiss went on and on and on. Became two. Then three. But when his hands roamed lower, cupping her bottom, then reached up to unzip her dress, she finally came to her senses.

Breathing heavily, she pushed at his chest. "No, Adam. No! I can't."

"Eve…" He tried to kiss her again.

She turned her face away, and the kiss landed on her cheek. "Please, Adam, don't. This is a mistake. A terrible mistake."

"Why is it a mistake? I want you, Eve. And I know you want me."

She couldn't deny that. She did want him. She wanted him more now than she had all those years ago. She wanted him so much she could hardly stand it. Fighting tears, she said, "What we want is not important. What will happen tomorrow and the next day is what matters."

"What are you talking about?"

"Adam, think about it. Your life is not here, but mine is. If we…if we make love now, everything will become more complicated and messy than it is already. There's…there's no point to it. No future for us. There never was."

"So that's it?" he said. "We're both free, you want me as much as I want you, but we're not going to do anything about it?"

"Yes, that's it." Straightening her dress, she picked up her recorder and phone and put them in her purse. Then, avoiding his eyes, she said, "I'm going to go now, Adam. Thank you for the interview."

Then she turned and, without looking back, walked out of the suite.

Adam wanted to go after her. He couldn't believe how little had changed. How much he still wanted her. It had been hard enough to leave her Saturday when everything in him had told him to open that door and follow her inside her little house, to then pick her up and carry her straight to her bedroom, where they could make love the entire night. If anything, the longing he'd felt then had only gotten stronger.

But much as he hated to admit it, Eve might be right. Her life *was* here, and his *was* somewhere else. And although he'd said he was free, he wasn't. Not really. First of all, there was Bethany. And even once he extricated himself from that relationship, there was still his career and all the people who depended upon that career.

He had commitments out the wazoo—not just the summer tour, but other bookings and possible bookings, including a television show in the works—which he had not told Eve about because he didn't want any word of it out there until the deal was finalized, if it ever was.

On top of that, there was his mother, and he really did want to try to get her to move to Nashville, so he could keep an eye on her. Then there was his place in LA. And if that television show worked out, he'd be spending more time there.

Lots of women might be interested in that kind of

nomadic life, but he doubted Eve was. She had two children. Young children. He couldn't imagine her wanting to uproot them or take them away from their father. The truth was, he and Eve were like shooting stars going in opposite directions.

So he didn't stop her when she walked out of the suite.

But he didn't have to like it.

Eve spent another sleepless night filled with fitful dreams. But the next morning, she determinedly put them and all thoughts of Adam and what might have been out of her mind and concentrated her energies on writing the best, most objective story about him she possibly could.

Joan loved it. "Is he as nice as you've painted him?" she asked after reading it.

Eve smiled. "He is."

"Not arrogant or obnoxious?"

"Not in the least."

"You two were in the same graduating class, right?"

"Yes."

"And you were friends?"

"Casual friends."

Joan cocked her head, studying Eve. "Nothing more?"

Eve shook her head. Hoped her voice or expression wouldn't betray her. "Nope. Nothing more."

"Was he as good-looking then as he is now?"

"He was always cute, but he was a loner. A bit weird. He didn't pay much attention to girls."

"Really?" Joan's expression was skeptical.

Eve knew Joan wasn't buying it, but too bad. Eve

had no intention of feeding her boss's curiosity, or anyone else's. She had her story and she was sticking to it.

"And all the girls accepted that?"

Eve shrugged. "I wouldn't know. I was kind of a loner myself."

Joan grinned. "We have that in common, don't we?"

Eve breathed an inner sigh of relief, glad she'd managed to steer Joan away from the subject of Adam.

"Well, thank you for a great article," Joan said. "And for the pictures."

For the rest of the afternoon, Eve wondered whether she should call Bill and tell him about seeing Adam again—and why. But something stopped her. The interview had been part of her job, and Bill would know that. She didn't owe him an explanation.

The story about Adam ran in Thursday's edition, on the front page of the Lifestyle section, under Eve's byline. And even though Eve had been telling herself Bill would be fine with it, she wasn't really surprised to receive a phone call from him that afternoon.

"I thought we had a meeting of the minds," he said tightly.

So he was angry. "We do. But I had no choice in the matter of the interview."

"You could have gotten out of it."

"And just how would I have managed that?" Now *she* was getting angry.

"If you'd wanted to, you'd have figured out something."

"You know, Bill, you're being unfair. I'm very lucky to still have a job. So when Joan asked me personally to do the interview, I didn't think it would be wise to try to fob it off on someone else."

The silence that followed was pregnant with tension. Finally, he said, "Tell me the truth, Eve. Are you going to see him again?"

"No. And I told him that."

Another silence. But this time, when he spoke, his voice had softened. "Okay. Thank you."

After they'd hung up, Eve gathered up her things and prepared to leave the office. She felt absurdly close to tears and too upset to face any more questions or congratulatory or curious calls from anyone else. For about the dozenth time since Adam had returned to Crandall Lake she asked herself why. Why had this happened? Why? And when would Adam leave so that her life could go back to normal?

You're kidding yourself. It'll never go back to normal, not now that you've seen Adam again. Not now that you know you've never really gotten over him. And especially not now that you know he feels the same way about you.

And yet… What could she do about any of it? No amount of thinking or bargaining with the heavens was going to change her situation. Seeing Adam, lying to herself that they might still have a chance to build a life together, was folly. Very dangerous folly.

The twins were number one in her life. Their happiness and security were more important than anything or anyone else. And there was no changing the circumstances of their birth or the bargain she'd made with Bill. She had no choice but to forget about Adam—again.

By the time Friday rolled around, and Bill had picked up the twins for the jaunt to Houston and their cousin's birthday weekend, Eve had finally managed to come to some kind of acceptance of the situation with Adam. She hated the phrase "it is what it is," but that fit her life to a T.

And now she was facing another lonely weekend that she'd have to fill somehow…and fill without going anyplace where she might bump into Adam again.

She decided the smart thing to do was to work all weekend. In fact, if she did that, if she wrote a couple of blogs ahead, and did as much research and prep work on a couple of articles hanging fire from Penny's departure, she might be able to take a few days off next week. Maybe take the twins somewhere for a long weekend. They'd love that. She could even invite her mother to come along.

So at eight the next morning, she was already at the paper, sitting at her desk and working on blog ideas. Her mother had invited her to come over for lunch, and tonight she would order takeout for dinner, then work late. And tomorrow she had church in the morning, and if necessary, she could come back into the office for the afternoon. Or, if she got desperate to do something else, she could go to a movie. And Bill was bringing the twins home by six. The weekend would be tolerable.

At twelve fifteen she saved her work, took her purse out of her desk drawer and waved goodbye to the two coworkers who were also there. "I'll be back in a couple of hours," she said.

She blinked as she walked out into the sunshine and put on her sunglasses. Heading for her car, which was parked in the small lot next to the building housing the paper, she didn't at first see the man leaning against her car. When she did, her heart did a somersault.

It was Adam.

"Hey," he said, straightening and giving her his sexy, crooked grin. Today he wore the black biker boots, weathered-looking jeans and a gray T-shirt that was inscribed Peace, Love, Music. The bad boy grown up.

"What are you doing here?" she said.

"I was driving by and saw your car."

She couldn't see his eyes, which were hidden by reflective sunglasses. "So?"

"So since it's almost lunchtime, I was waiting to see if you'd come out. If not, I was going to go in and get you."

"Why? Wh-what do you want?" She hated how she'd stammered. How he seemed to reduce her insides to a bowlful of jelly.

"Just to say thanks for the great article you wrote. And I wanted to take you to lunch."

"You're welcome, on the article. But I can't go to lunch with you. My mother's expecting me. She made stuffed cabbage rolls because she knows how much I love them." Now, *why* had she said that? She was an idiot.

"Stuffed cabbage rolls!" He gave her a wicked grin. "I'll go with *you*, then."

Eve stared at him. Go *with* her? She opened her mouth to say she didn't remember inviting him, but before she could, his grin grew even wider, and even though she couldn't see his eyes, she knew they were twinkling. Oh, he was pleased with himself. Childishly, she felt like kicking him.

"C'mon, Eve. What's the big deal? It's just lunch. Anyway, don't you think it's *time* I met your mother?"

Eve swallowed. She felt helpless in the face of his

audacity. His assurance that she wouldn't deny him. That whatever he wanted, she'd go along with it.

And the truth was, she didn't *want* to say no to him ever—about anything. And he knew it. He'd known it on Tuesday when she'd said she wasn't going to see him again. And he knew it now. She could hear the knowledge in his voice. She wondered if he also knew how her heart was hammering, and how weak with desire she felt. Oh, God, she was a mess.

"I'll drive," he said, knowing he'd won. He inclined his head, and she saw a red Porsche convertible parked at the curb. He laughed at her expression. "Yeah, I traded in the other rental yesterday. Figured if I was gonna be here awhile, I might as well drive something fun."

Eve knew this was crazy. Utterly and completely crazy. But at that moment, she was powerless to stop herself. When he reached for her hand, she gave it to him, and she let him lead her to the car and help her in.

"Your mom still live in the same house?" he asked when he climbed into the driver's seat and started the car.

"Yes," she said weakly. Dear God. What would her mother *think* when she saw him?

Eve didn't have long to wonder. Less than ten minutes later he swung into the driveway of her mother's house. Almost instantly, her mother opened the door. Eve wished she could take a photo of the astounded expression on Anna's face when she realized who the man was walking to the door with her daughter. When her mother's eyes met Eve's, Eve saw a dozen questions reflected in them.

I'm in for it now. What in the world am I going to

*tell her when she starts asking those questions? And
wanting them answered?*

Well, it was too late to worry about that problem.
Now she'd better concentrate on giving the best performance of her life, and worry about the rest of it after
she'd survived lunch.

Chapter Seven

"I hope you don't mind another mouth to feed, Mrs. Cermak," Adam said.

"Of course I don't mind," Anna said.

"I dropped by the paper to invite Eve to lunch, and when she said she was coming here and that you'd made cabbage rolls, I invited myself along."

When Adam gave Anna his famous smile, Eve could see her mother beginning to melt. "Well, come on in," she said.

As always, her mother's small bungalow was spotless. The furniture gleamed with polish, the air smelled like lemon Pledge and there wasn't a speck of dust anywhere. A vase of fresh flowers adorned the small gateleg table in the entryway, and the grandfather clock that Anna had inherited from her parents chimed the half hour from its place of honor in the corner. As they walked back into the bright red-and-white kitchen, they were greeted with wonderful smells. Eve smiled when she saw Daisy, her mother's calico cat, snoozing in the bay window overlooking the backyard. The cat barely opened one eye at their entrance, then settled back into her comfortable nap.

"If I'd known Eve was bringing a guest, I'd've set the dining room table," Anna fretted, giving Eve an accusatory glance.

"This is better. I like eating in the kitchen," Adam said.

Eve's mother hurriedly set a third place, and invited them to sit. Eve said she'd get them something to drink, and when Adam said yes to iced tea, she went to the fridge and took out the pitcher her mother always had on hand. By the time she'd poured them each a glass, Anna had put the food out. Eve and Adam were seated across from each other at the round table, with her mother between them.

Adam took a generous helping of cabbage rolls and mashed potatoes and immediately dug in. "This is wonderful stuff," he said after a couple of mouthfuls. "I haven't had them since I was a kid."

Anna beamed. Nothing made her happier than feeding people.

Eve knew her mother was dying to ask questions, but she tried to forestall her by saying, "Did you read the article I wrote about Adam in Thursday's paper, Mom?"

"I did. It was really good."

"I thought so," Adam said. "Your daughter made me sound a lot nicer than I am."

"Oh, I'm sure that's not true," Anna said. "She tells

me you two were in the same high school graduating class?"

"Yes, we were." Adam's eyes met Eve's across the table. "What else did she tell you?"

Anna frowned a little. She looked at Eve.

Eve hated the way she blushed. Now she *really* wanted to kick Adam. What was he *doing*?

"Was there something else to tell?" Anna said, turning her blue-eyed gaze back to Adam.

"You know how it is with teenagers, Mrs. Cermak," Adam said, chuckling. "They never tell their parents everything."

I'll kill him, Eve thought. *I will cheerfully kill him.* "He's teasing you, Mom. We, uh, hung out together our senior year. It was kind of…group dating. You know."

"Group dating? Really? You never said."

Eve knew she was *really* in for it when her mother got her alone again, because both her parents had always believed she'd been totally honest with them. She could see even more questions in her mother's eyes, the dawning awareness that maybe her daughter had hidden more than one thing from her.

"She probably knew you wouldn't approve of me," Adam said. "I was kind of a wild kid."

"Were you?"

"Yeah. My dad took off when I was pretty young, and I acted out a lot."

"That must have been hard on you." Anna's voice had softened in sympathy.

Adam shrugged. "I survived. It made me tough."

"I don't think you're tough. I think you just pretend to be tough." Her mother smiled. "Anyway, you've certainly made something of your life now."

"I've been lucky."

"It takes more than luck to accomplish what you have."

How did he do it? Eve wondered. Every female who came within ten feet of him fell under his spell. She knew darned well her mother would have had a stroke if Eve had told her about him during their high school days, but here she was now, completely charmed by him.

Soon her mother was asking him all kinds of questions about his family and his career.

"Your mother must be so proud of you," she finally said.

"I hope so," he said. "I've tried to be a good son."

"From what I hear, you've been a wonderful son."

"Thank you."

"And you've never married?"

"No. I only came close once." His gaze sought Eve's. "But she got away," he added softly.

Eve's heart skipped and she looked down at her plate.

"I'm sure you wouldn't have any problem finding someone now," Anna said.

Adam laughed. "I'm picky. I want somebody who can cook like you do! This is the best meal I've had in a long time."

"You're welcome to come and eat here anytime you like. That hospital food is horrible. I'm sure you're sick of it."

"My mother's actually out of the hospital and in rehab now."

"Even so. I'm sure she won't be cooking anytime

soon." Anna turned to Eve. "Bring him to lunch on Wednesday. I'm making pierogies."

"Pierogies!" Adam said. "You don't have to ask me twice! I'll be here."

Eve knew her mother had no idea what she was doing to Eve or to her resolve to stay away from Adam. If Anna only knew the Pandora's box she was flirting with.

Eve had to wait before she could gracefully find a reason to leave, but fifteen minutes later she figured it was okay to say, "Mom, I've got to get back to the paper. I still have a ton of stuff to do this weekend before the twins get home again."

At the door, Anna embraced Adam. "I'm so glad you came."

"I am, too." He kissed her cheek, saying softly, "I wish I'd known you when I was young."

"I wish that, too." Anna gave Eve another reproachful look.

Eve squirmed, her guilty feelings almost overwhelming her. Had she misjudged her parents? *Would* they have accepted Adam years ago?

As she and Adam walked outside, Adam said, "Thanks for letting me come. I really enjoyed myself."

"I'm sure you did," Eve said drily. "Another notch in your belt."

Adam gave her a sidelong look. "Think so?"

Eve shook her head. "Don't play dumb. You've won my mother over and you know it."

He chuckled softly and opened the passenger door of the Porsche to help her in. "Now all I have to do is win *you* over."

* * *

Eve half expected Adam to try to talk her into spending more time with him that weekend, but surprisingly, he didn't. He dropped her back at the paper, thanked her again, said he'd call her before Wednesday and took off. She knew she should be grateful—wasn't that what she *wanted*? Yet perversely, she was disappointed.

She didn't hear from him on Sunday, either. She told herself that was good. She did manage to get a lot of work done, just as she'd planned. So maybe she would ask Joan for Thursday and Friday off and take the twins somewhere for a really long weekend.

As promised, Bill brought Natalie and Nathan home at six. "They've already eaten," he said. "We stopped for hamburgers on the way."

"Thanks."

"So how was your weekend?"

"Good. I got lots of work done."

"You gonna be at the office tomorrow?"

"Yes. The twins are spending the day with Olivia." Her cousin had Monday and Tuesday off this week.

"Can we have lunch? There's something I need to discuss with you."

"Sure. Noon?"

"How about one? I have an appointment at eleven thirty. Can we meet at Tony's?" Tony's was a favorite Italian restaurant near the paper's office.

"Okay."

After Bill left, Eve wondered what it was he wanted to talk about that he couldn't discuss in front of the twins. She hoped he wasn't going to throw another curveball at her about next weekend. If he did, she would just have to be firm about not letting him disrupt her plans again.

She was too busy Monday morning to spend much time thinking about what he might say, and before she knew it, it was twelve forty-five and time to head to Tony's to meet him.

Bill was already seated at a window table when she walked in. After greeting Rose, Tony's wife, who served as the hostess, Eve joined Bill. "So what's up?" she said.

"Let's wait and talk after we order."

Eve didn't like his solemn tone. It made her think his news wasn't going to be something she'd be happy about.

After placing their orders, he leaned forward. "On Wednesday, I'm leaving for California. I'll be on assignment out there for at least six weeks."

Eve blinked. "You're kidding."

"No, I'm not. It's sudden, I know."

"I guess." Eve's thoughts were beginning to whirl. Bill being gone for six weeks was going to throw the entire summer schedule into chaos. Part of her was thrilled she'd have the twins all to herself for the bulk of the summer. The other part of her worried how she'd manage. Would her mother help her out? But hadn't her mother said something about going to a bridge tournament next month?

"The whole family's going," Bill continued, "and I want to take the twins with us."

Eve's mouth fell open and she shook her head reflexively.

"Eve, before you say no, at least *listen* to me. The company has rented a house for us that's only a block from the beach. The twins will love it out there. And you won't have to worry about finding things for them to do this summer. They'll be safe and having fun, and you'll be free to work."

"But—"

"You can even come out and join us one weekend. Missy said to invite you." He smiled at her. "I know this is a shock, and you haven't had any time to think about it, but it's a terrific opportunity for the twins. They'll have a wonderful summer if you let them."

Although Eve hated to admit it, she knew Bill was right. She gave a few more halfhearted objections, but in the end, she agreed. And before lunch was over, she also agreed to pack everything the twins would need the next day. They would spend Tuesday night with Bill because their flight to California was leaving early Wednesday morning.

As she headed back to the office, she realized fate had handed her a gift. With the twins gone, if she wanted to see Adam, she could. He wouldn't see them, so there'd be no danger he'd ever put two and two together. This was an opportunity for her to get him out of her system. Then, by the time the twins returned from California, he would be long gone.

And Eve's secret would still be safe.

That night, as Eve was helping Natalie pack—she'd already gotten Nathan's things ready and he was happily playing an online game—Natalie said, "Janie Logan's mom told me that you know Adam Crenshaw. Is that true, Mom?"

Eve gave an inward sigh. Looked down into her daughter's eyes—eyes that would never allow Eve to forget how and when her children had been conceived—and said in as casual a tone as she could manage, "Yes, honey, that's true."

"Janie said he's here, in Crandall Lake."

"Yes. His mother's been sick, so he came home."

"Why didn't you *tell* me?"

Eve pretended to be amused by forcing a chuckle. "*Tell* you? It wasn't that important."

"Not important! Mom! Adam *Crenshaw*? He's the lead singer in Version II! I *love* him! And you *know* him! I can't believe we're going to California and I won't get to meet him!"

"Natalie, it's not a big d—"

"Can you call him up? Maybe ask him to come over tonight? So I can meet him before I leave?"

"No. I can't just—"

"Please? All the kids are talking about him. Janie even *saw* him at the store the other day. And they all know that you know him. It's not *fair*! I didn't even know you'd written a story about him until Janie told me. I felt so stupid."

Now Eve did sigh. "Look, honey, I'm sorry I didn't say anything about him, but really, I—I just didn't think it was important."

"You said that already. And it *is* important. He's one of the biggest stars *ever*. And he's from *here*. And you *know* him." Natalie's voice had gone from a wail punctuated with exclamation points to injured disbelief at her mother's ignorance.

"I'm sorry, Natalie. I guess I'm out of it." Eve realized she should have known the twins were bound to hear about Adam. After all, the whole town was buzzing about him.

"So will you call him? Please, Mom, please? I just want to be able to tell my friends I've met him. If I could get a selfie with him my friends would *die*!"

"I can't do that, honey. He spends most of his time at the rehab center with his mother. Besides, it's late."

Natalie looked at Eve as if she had two heads. "It's only nine o'clock."

"I'm sorry to disappoint you, but I'm not calling him."

"Mom!"

"Please don't argue, Natalie. It won't change anything."

Natalie's eyes filled with tears as she stared at Eve. "This is so not fair!"

Eve thought about resorting to that old standby, "Who told you life was going to be fair?" but thought better of it when she saw how upset her daughter was. "Sweetheart, I can't call him tonight, but I'll tell you what. If he's still in town when you get back from California, I'll invite him over so you can meet him."

Natalie glared at her. "He'll probably be gone by then."

That was what Eve was counting on. "Maybe not."

Natalie swiped her tears away and heaved an exaggerated sigh. But to Eve's relief, she didn't argue further.

Eve knew she'd managed to dodge a bullet—a huge one—*and* one she should have seen coming. She should be happy. And yet, some perverse part of her *wanted* Adam to meet the twins. She guessed she would always wonder what he would think about them. If he would have any idea they were his. When she looked at them, she always saw Adam in them. Yet no one else had ever guessed. Not even her mother, and her mother adored them and spent as much time with them as she could. Even Saturday, when her mother had seen Adam up close and personal, she hadn't seemed overly suspicious or concerned. Sure, she'd been surprised to find Eve had hidden her "group dating" from her, but Eve knew her mother was smart enough to realize most kids were secretive about anything they thought their parents would disapprove of. Anna hadn't seemed to attach too much significance to the revelation. If she had, she wouldn't have hesitated to question Eve.

Later, after the twins were in bed and, hopefully, asleep, Eve poured herself a glass of iced tea and went out to the front porch to unwind and think about everything.

Was she doing the right thing contemplating seeing more of Adam? Wouldn't it be smarter—and *safer*— to stay as far away from him as possible, whether the twins were around or not? But these weeks while they were in California might be the only time she'd ever be able to have with Adam. Didn't she deserve at least that much? She knew they could never have any kind of ongoing relationship, but surely there could be no harm in grabbing this little bit of happiness.

She bit her lip. *Is this too much to ask?*

She guessed, in the end, the real question was: if she did continue to see him, if what there was between them continued to grow, would she be strong enough to walk away from him again?

Because Adam's mother was doing really well and Austin had assured him it was okay to go back to Nashville and take care of the things hanging fire, Adam booked a flight for Thursday. He would stay a couple of days—have the interview with *Rolling Stone*, meet with his agent and his producer, talk to his bandmates and have his overdue discussion with Bethany. Then he'd be free to come home. "Why not go tomorrow?" Austin asked. The two brothers were in Austin's condo, having a beer after sharing some take-out Italian.

"I have a lunch date tomorrow."

"Can't you reschedule?"

Adam heard the curiosity in Austin's voice. "I've been invited to the home of an old friend, and I don't want to disappoint her." He grinned. "She's making pierogies."

Austin chuckled. "I'm guessing that invitation was irresistible. So is she pretty?"

"She looks darned good for a seventy-year-old woman."

Austin frowned. "Who is she?"

"The mother of an old friend."

"Is that old friend by any chance a hot blonde reporter?"

Adam just smiled.

"What's the story there?"

"Eve and I dated in high school."

"Eve?" Austin laughed.

"What's so funny?"

"Adam…and Eve. You don't think that's funny?"

Adam rolled his eyes.

"So I'm guessing you still like her?"

"Never stopped," Adam admitted. "Just didn't know she was available."

"And now you do."

"Yeah."

"Is it serious?"

"Don't know yet."

"But you'd like it to be?"

"Don't know that yet, either."

"What about Bethany?"

Adam sighed. Took a swallow of his beer. "I'm gonna take care of that this week."

Austin made a face. "She's not gonna be happy."

"I know."

"My guess is she's been thinking wedding bells."

"I know."

"You gonna keep her on as your publicist?"

"We'll see. Depends how she takes the news. Whether she wants to stay on or not."

"Well, good luck, bro."

"Thanks. I'm gonna need it."

Anna had worked all day Tuesday making the pierogies, frying up the onions in butter that she would serve with them, and topping off all her efforts with the nut kolache she always prepared for holidays and special occasions. She figured this lunch today, with Adam Crenshaw as her guest, was a very special occasion.

Anna couldn't believe how blind she'd been. She'd always known the marriage between Eve and Bill wasn't the perfect match both she and Bill's mother had pretended it to be. Had *wanted* it to be.

First of all, there was the shock of the twins being born too early. And even though none of them—not Anna's beloved Joe nor Bill's father, William—and certainly not Anna or Ellen Ruth—had ever spoken their doubts aloud, Anna knew all four parents had seen the ripples in the surface of their children's marriage.

In the beginning, after Anna had gotten over the shock that her dutiful and obedient Eve—a child who had never given her one moment's worry—had hidden something so important from her, she had been happy about their marriage. She and Joe had been disappointed that college for Eve would have to be postponed, but after all, she was now married to Bill. And hadn't Anna and Ellen Ruth always hoped and prayed for this outcome? Anna loved Bill like a son, and now her daughter loved him, too.

But very early on, something seemed wrong. Lacking. Anna had glimpsed something in her daughter's eyes, something that disturbed her. And Eve had never acted like a young woman madly in love. She had acted more like a settled wife who was a comfortable friend to her partner. Where was the passion? Anna had asked herself. She'd often seen Bill put his arm around Eve or give her a kiss or a look, but she'd never once seen Eve do the same in return.

Anna had tried to talk to Eve about her marriage, but Eve wouldn't confide in her. All she would say was "We have some problems, but we're working on them, Mom. Don't worry."

Don't worry.

As if any mother who loved her child could *stop* worrying when she knew her child was in trouble.

And then came the day when Eve had told them she and Bill were divorcing. Joe had actually cried that night, but he was already sick with his cancer, and his emotions were close to the surface. Anna had done her share of crying, too, but what could she do?

The only good thing was that the divorce was as amicable as it was possible for a divorce to be. Bill and Eve had remained friends, and there seemed to be no animosity between them. Even the shared custody of the twins hadn't seemed to cause problems—or at least, not many.

But *now*.

What would happen now?

Eve might not suspect Anna had discovered her secret, because Anna had taken care not to give her daughter any reason to, but all Anna had had to do was see those gray eyes of Adam Crenshaw's, and she'd felt as if someone had punched her in the stomach.

She'd known instantly.

Did Bill?

Or had Eve deceived him the way she'd deceived her parents? Surely not. And yet, maybe she hadn't had to say anything. Bill had always loved Eve—that had been apparent from the time they were kids. Maybe Bill had seen his chance to have Eve and taken it.

And what about Adam? Did *he* know about the twins? Anna didn't think so. He couldn't have been that good an actor, to come into her home, to pretend. No. He didn't know. So that meant Eve had never told him she was pregnant.

Why not? Had she thought he wouldn't want to marry her? He hadn't struck Anna as the type of person who would have abandoned her, and yet he *had* gone away and left her behind. When Anna had asked him about his start in the music business, he'd told her he'd left Crandall Lake the moment he'd earned his high school diploma. He hadn't even stayed for graduation.

Anna's heart ached as she thought about what it must have been like for Eve when she'd realized she was pregnant. If only she'd felt she could tell Anna.

Anna wanted to weep when she realized how desperate Eve had probably felt.

I let her down.

The knowledge made Anna determined to learn the entire story. And equally determined to get to know the father of her grandchildren.

Chapter Eight

It was hard to say goodbye to the twins, but Eve knew their departure for California was the best thing for everyone. After promises to Skype or do FaceTime calls every night and assurances they'd be texting back and forth and sending lots of pictures, they kissed and hugged and said their "I love yous" and Eve finally let them go.

After that, she moped around for a while, then told herself to put on her big-girl panties and get to work.

The morning at the paper passed quickly, and before she knew it, it was noon and time to leave for her mother's. She and Adam had agreed to meet there. When she arrived, she saw his car parked out front. She knocked on the front door, then let herself in. She could hear him and her mother laughing in the kitchen. Her heart squeezed at the sound.

"Everything smells awfully good," she said when she entered the kitchen.

Her mother, standing at the stove warming the pierogies, turned and smiled.

Adam, sitting at the table with a glass of lemonade in front of him, grinned up at her. "Doesn't it? I can't wait." His eyes swept her, taking in her slim black pants and red crocheted top with an appreciative look.

He didn't look so bad himself. But then, he never did. He was one of those fortunate men who wore his clothes with a casual elegance, whether dressed in faded denim as he was today, or in a tux, as he had been in so many of the photos she'd seen over the years.

"Did the kids get off okay?" her mother asked.

"Yes. They were so excited."

"Where were they going?" Adam asked.

Eve explained.

"That means I'm not going to get to meet them," he said. "I'm disappointed."

"My daughter was disappointed about that, too," Eve said. "She tried to get me to call you last night. She wanted bragging rights with her friends."

"You should have."

Eve shrugged. "It was late."

"I'm a night owl."

"Natalie has to learn when I say no, it means no."

"Some of us have a hard time with that," he said, laughing.

Eve couldn't help grinning in return. She remembered that about him. How could she not? She'd never been able to say no to him.

Anna turned off the heat under the pierogies and

transferred them to a serving platter. The platter joined a small serving bowl containing a tomato-and-cucumber salad, which was already on the table.

As they ate, Adam told Anna about his mother's progress. "She's doing so well I'm going to fly back to Nashville tomorrow."

Eve's heart contracted. The disappointment she felt was so acute, she was afraid it showed on her face.

"I won't be gone long, though," he said. "I just have some things I have to take care of in person, then I'll be back. In fact—" he turned to look at Eve "—I'm thinking of spending the rest of the summer here."

Now her heart jumped. "Really?"

"Yeah. I'm going to give the guys in the band a month's vacation, then have them come here to get ready for our tour. In the meantime, I'll have to find somewhere suitable to practice. I'll get Marty—my manager—to start looking."

"You can probably find something in Austin," Eve said.

"That's what I figured."

"Why are you going to all that trouble?" Anna asked.

He grinned. "Two reasons. I discovered I like being here. And I want to keep a closer eye on my mother."

Eve's mind was racing. Bill would have a fit when he realized Adam was going to be around for such a long time. He would jump to the conclusion that Eve was somehow involved in Adam's decision. Had she been? She was still trying to think of something to say when Adam's cell phone rang.

He quickly looked at it, then said, "I'd better take this. I'm sorry."

"It's okay," Anna said. "You go ahead."

He answered the phone, said, "Hold on a minute, Marty," then pushed his chair back and walked out of the room. Eve avoided her mother's eyes and continued eating. She could hear Adam talking in a low tone but not what he was saying.

He was back a few seconds later. "Sorry," he said again. "That was my manager. He's found a studio in Austin that we can rent the month of August, and even use in September until our concert date there."

"That's good news," Anna said.

Eve wondered what her mother would say if she knew the truth. She doubted her mother would be so enthusiastic if she had any idea that Adam's presence could jeopardize her grandchildren's happy and settled lives. For the remainder of lunch, Eve was unable to relax again or to enjoy being there. All she could think about was how Bill was going to react to the news and how she was going to avoid Adam meeting the twins.

Finally lunch was over. Anna insisted on packing up some of the kolache and sending it off with Adam. "Do you want some, too, honey?" she asked Eve.

"Sure. Thanks."

Eve knew Adam had noticed she wasn't herself because he kept giving her curious looks. Her mother had noticed, too, and Eve knew she'd be subjected to a few uncomfortable questions later on. She guessed she'd better figure out how to answer them.

In the meantime, all Eve wanted was to get out of there. Thank God she hadn't ridden with Adam and could go off in her own car where she could think straight. And maybe, if she was lucky, some miraculous answer would come to her about how to avoid the possible disaster Adam's continued presence might bring about.

Adam had intended to deal with all the other things he had on his plate in Nashville before having his talk with Bethany, but she forced his hand by showing up at his house a little after eleven o'clock Thursday night.

If he could have pretended not to be there, he would have, because the last thing he wanted was to have what was sure to be an emotional confrontation with her when he was tired from the long day. He'd planned to pour himself a drink to unwind and then hit the sack. Unfortunately, the lights were all on and she could see he was home.

He sighed wearily and opened the door. "Hey," he said. "I was gonna suggest we get together in the morning."

"Sweetie, I couldn't wait that long. You've been gone for weeks! And I missed you." She threw her arms around his neck and kissed him.

Adam couldn't stop the flinch that was automatic.

She drew back and stared at him.

The silence seemed deafening, and Bethany's green eyes hardened as their gazes locked. "I thought so," she said, stepping back.

"Bethany…"

"Don't try to deny it." Her mouth twisted into an ugly line. "Who is she?"

Adam sighed. "Look, there is no 'she.'"

"Oh, really? I wasn't born yesterday, Adam. I've known for a while now that something was wrong, so don't try to give me any bull—"

"There *is no she*. What we had, you and me, it...
it just ran its course. I know I should have talked to
you about this weeks ago, but I kept putting it off. I'm
sorry." When she said nothing, just continued to give
him an icy glare of disbelief, he plunged ahead. "It's
not you. It's me."

"You know," she said tightly, "that old line, 'it's not
you, it's me' is insulting. At least be man enough to
say what you really feel. You're tired of me. You want
to move on to something new, so you're dumping me.
And if there's no one else *at the moment*, there probably will be tomorrow. I mean, hell, Adam. All you
have to do is crook your little finger and women will
be jumping into your bed."

Adam had never felt like such a heel. She had a
right to be angry.

"Are you firing me as your publicist, too?" she de-
manded.

"I don't want to. You're the best there is." That
wasn't completely true. She was *one* of the best, and
he would prefer someone else now, but it would be
wiser to wait and see how things worked out. Maybe
she would decide on her own that a continuing business relationship would be too awkward.

She studied him a few seconds longer, an unreadable
expression in her eyes, then shrugged. "Okay, then."
Opening her purse, she took out the separate key ring
with the keys to his house and the card for the security gate. She tossed them on the table in the entryway.
"What time do you want to meet tomorrow to go over
your publicity agenda?"

They settled on eleven in the morning at his Music
Row office.

They said a strained goodbye, and once more, there was something in her eyes that bothered Adam, something that said he hadn't heard the last of this.

As she turned to leave, Adam followed her outside and stood on the top of the wide, shallow steps leading up to the front door. He watched as she got into her BMW and drove down the long drive to the gated entrance. Although a person needed a gate card to enter, all you had to do to exit was drive up to the gate and it would open. After the gate closed behind her, Adam continued to stand there until the taillights of her car had disappeared around a copse of trees. Only then did he turn, walk inside and lock the door behind him.

Part of him was relieved the ordeal of breaking the news to her was over. The other part of him, the cautious, skeptical part honed after years of hard work and experience in a tough business, knew breaking it off with Bethany had been too easy.

That look in her eyes, the one he couldn't interpret, had meant something.

And that something wasn't anything good.

Eve generally talked to her mother every day or so. Sometimes the calls only lasted a couple of minutes—just a quick "how are you?" Or a "can I pick up anything for you when I'm at the supermarket?" So she wasn't surprised, but she *was* prepared when her mother phoned on Friday.

"Are you going to be home tonight?" her mother said when Eve answered.

"I'm planning to. Why?"

"I thought I'd stop by for a while."

Eve immediately knew she was in for a grilling. For

a moment, she wished she'd said she had plans, but what was the sense of putting her mother off? Sooner or later, Eve had to answer her mother's questions. Might as well get it over with. "Why don't you come for dinner? I'm fixing salmon."

"I'd love to. Can I bring anything?"

"No, I'm good. I have stuff for salad, and there's some rosemary bread in the freezer. I'm at the paper, but I'll be home by six."

By the time Anna arrived, Eve was ready for her. She knew exactly what she was going to tell her mother. And what she wasn't. And she'd also decided she would not be the one to bring up Adam's name. She would let her mother introduce the subject.

Her mother waited until they were seated at the table and had begun to eat. She complimented Eve on the food, then said lightly, as if it wasn't really important, "I enjoyed having Adam for lunch Wednesday."

"Good." Eve smiled. "I think he enjoyed it, too. I *know* he enjoyed the food!"

Anna's blue eyes were thoughtful as they met Eve's across the table. "He's a nice man. Much nicer than I would have imagined."

"He *is* nice." Eve reached for a piece of bread and took a bite of her salad.

"I have to admit," her mother continued, "I was a bit shocked to find out you'd dated him in high school. I thought I knew everything you were doing and everyone you knew."

It took every bit of willpower Eve possessed to keep her voice light, and she prayed she wouldn't blush or stammer and betray herself. "I'm sorry, Mom, that I didn't tell you about Adam. I knew you'd never let me go out with him. And...I wanted to." She gave her mother a sheepish smile. "I was a kid. He seemed exciting then."

"*Then?* He's exciting *now.* Don't you think?"

What was her mother up to? This wasn't the way Eve had imagined this conversation. "Yes, of course," she answered slowly. "He's a big star. But I'm no longer a naive young girl."

Anna didn't answer immediately—just took a bite of salmon, then blotted her mouth with her napkin. When her eyes met Eve's again, an emotion was reflected in their depths that made Eve's heart lurch. "I'm not naive, either, Eve."

Eve swallowed. To give herself time to think, she picked up her water glass and took a long drink. When she set the glass back down, her hand was shaking, and she hurriedly put it in her lap to hide it. Although she wanted to look anywhere but there, she couldn't manage to tear her gaze from her mother's. Time seemed to stand still, and every sound was heightened: the tick of the wall clock, the roar of a lawn mower somewhere nearby, the distant honk of a horn, the hum of her refrigerator, her own breathing.

Anna finally broke the silence. "Does Bill know?"

The quiet question affected Eve like a pin stuck into a balloon. She sank back against her chair, and didn't even try to stop the tears that erupted.

"Oh, sweetheart!" Her mother jumped up and walked around the table. Crouching, she put her arms around Eve.

Eve wanted to stop crying, but for so long she'd kept such a tight lid on her emotions. Her mother's simple question had unleashed something inside Eve, something filled with pain and regret and desire and sorrow. Something she might never again be able to pretend didn't exist.

"It's okay...it's okay," her mother kept saying.

But it wasn't okay. It hadn't been okay since the day she'd chosen to let Adam go.

Her mother's arms tightened around her and she kissed the top of her head. "Eve, honey, I'm so sorry. I didn't mean to upset you like this. I love you. You know that, don't you?"

It took a while, but Eve finally ran out of tears. When she took a long, shuddering breath, her mother released her and stood. "Do you want me to leave?"

Eve looked up. She must be a mess, because she wasn't a pretty crier. Her face got blotchy and red, and her eyes swelled up. She shook her head. "No. I—I want to talk about this."

"Are you sure?"

Eve saw concern—and love. She did not see condemnation. "Yes, I'm sure."

Anna went back to her seat across from Eve. Eve blew her nose in the tissues her mother had handed her, took another long breath, pushed her plate—with her dinner still half-uneaten—away and said, "I'll answer your question first. Yes. Bill knows."

"About Adam? Or about the twins?"

"Both."

"What about Adam? Does *he* know about the twins?"

"No. And he can't."

"But—"

"I know, Mom. It doesn't seem right, does it? But I promised Bill I'd never tell Adam. That was the deal we made when he offered to marry me."

"But I don't understand. What happened? Why didn't you tell Adam? Did you think he *wouldn't* marry you?"

"I didn't know I was pregnant until after he'd been gone awhile." Eve sighed again, then decided to begin at the beginning. She told her mother everything then, how she had fallen in love with Adam their senior year, how she'd kept their relationship a secret from everyone, how Adam had wanted her to go away with him the night before their graduation ceremony, how she was going to until Anna and Joe had given her the locket and said the things they'd said, how she just couldn't do it after that—couldn't break their hearts. She told Anna how she'd cried and cried, then how she'd realized she was pregnant and how she'd panicked and tried to reach Adam, but how he never answered his cell phone.

"I really panicked then," Eve said. "I didn't know where he was. I had no way of getting in touch with him."

"But what about his family? Why didn't you call his mother?"

"How could I? They didn't know me."

"So what? All you had to do was say you were a friend." Anna frowned. "I mean, if you *loved* Adam…"

"I thought…I thought you and Daddy would be…" She stopped. "I—I guess I…wasn't…brave enough." That was the truth of it. That was *exactly* why she hadn't called his mother. She'd been a coward all the way around. Too afraid to tell her parents about Adam. Too afraid to face the consequences of what she'd done. Too afraid to take a chance on Adam and how he'd react to having to abandon his dreams. Instead, she'd grabbed the lifeline Bill had offered. The safe route.

All these years.

All these years she'd been lying to herself.

Telling herself she'd done the only thing she could do. Telling herself she'd protected her children and her parents. Telling herself she'd been sensible and practical, that she'd made a mature decision by thinking of others instead of herself.

Instead, she'd simply been a coward.

She'd cheated Adam, she'd cheated Bill and she'd cheated her children. *Adam's children.*

All these thoughts and more tumbled in her mind. Eve stared at her mother. What was her mother thinking? Was she as ashamed of Eve as Eve was herself?

"Oh, Eve," her mother finally said. The sadness on her face made Eve want to weep again.

Eve looked away. What was there to say? She'd messed up her life. She'd messed up a lot of lives.

"So what does Bill say now that Adam's come back?"

"He's upset. He doesn't want me to see him."

"He's afraid you'll tell him about Nathan and Natalie."

"Yes."

Again, silence reigned for long seconds. Then Anna sighed. "Tell me something, Eve. Do you *want* to see Adam?"

"Yes."

"And he wants to see you."

"I think so. Yes."

"I think so, too. I think he acts like a man in love."

"I—I haven't heard from him since Wednesday." She didn't add how many times she'd looked at her phone and willed it to ring, then prayed that it wouldn't. Or how many times she'd wondered what she'd do if it *did* ring. And what she'd do if it didn't.

"Well, he said he had a lot of things to take care of in Nashville," her mother pointed out. "I'm sure he'll call."

Eve grimaced. "Even if he does, wouldn't it be better for everybody concerned if I don't see him again? I mean, what's the point? There's no future for us."

"Are you sure? If you love each other…"

"I don't know that he loves me. I know he *wants* me, but maybe that's just to prove something to himself."

Her mother sat thinking, then sighed. "How will you know unless you keep seeing him?"

Eve nodded. That was the crux of the problem, wasn't it? She was damned if she did and damned if she didn't. "What do you think I should do, Mom?"

"Oh, honey, I can't make that decision for you. No one can."

Eve knew that. She just didn't want to choose wrong again. "I don't have a great track record."

Her mother gave her a sad smile. "Important decisions aren't easy for anyone. Just know this. Whatever you decide to do, I'll support you one hundred percent."

"Even if my decision disrupts everyone's life? Including yours?"

"Even then."

Long after her mother had gone home, Eve sat thinking. It was after midnight when she finally headed for bed. She still wasn't sure what she'd do when she heard from Adam again. But at least now that her mother knew the truth, Eve didn't feel quite so alone.

Chapter Nine

Adam thought about calling Eve on Saturday to let her know he would be heading back to Crandall Lake on Monday. But he decided against it. Might be wise to cool it a bit. She'd made it pretty clear she didn't think seeing him again was a good idea. And if not for her mother's invitation to lunch on Wednesday, he wasn't sure he *would* have seen Eve again. Better to wait until they could meet face-to-face.

But he missed her. Being with Eve again had somehow erased all the years she had been gone from his life. He wondered if she realized the main reason he'd decided to spend the rest of the summer in Crandall Lake had a lot more to do with her than with his mother. Because he could have brought his mother back to Nashville. He'd actually broached the subject with her the night before he'd left, and she'd said she was willing to think about it.

Eve, though, was a different story. Adam knew, just from the little bit of time he'd been able to see her in the past few weeks, that he wanted to explore the possibility of an ongoing relationship. And it would be impossible to do that if he didn't stay in Crandall Lake. It wasn't as if Eve was free to come to Nashville or LA with him.

Her children were the big question mark.

He wished he'd had a chance to meet them before they'd left for California with their father. Once he was able to spend some time with them, he might be better able to predict whether they would be a giant stumbling block to a relationship with their mother or whether it might be possible to win them over. He'd already won Eve's mother over, or at least he thought he had.

So after considering everything, he didn't call her. He would simply go back to Crandall Lake and show up on her doorstep when he arrived. That way, the advantage would be his. Even if she *had* come to the conclusion it would be better not to see him again, she would have a hard time sending him away.

The twins texted Eve and sent pictures several times every day, and the three of them talked using Skype or FaceTime every night. Gradually, even though she missed them desperately, she got used to the idea of them being in California.

Because Bill had been right. They were having a wonderful time, and being out there with Bill and Melissa and little Will was good for them. Much better than spending the summer in Crandall Lake, where Eve would have been scrambling to find things for them to do while she worked.

Sitting at her desk at the paper on Monday, after they'd been gone five days, she chuckled as she remembered the previous night's phone call. The twins had spent the day at Universal Studios and were excitedly talking over each other to tell her about it.

"So you had a great time," she said when she could get a word in edgewise.

"The best part was the Jurassic Park ride! It was outstanding, Mom!" Nathan said.

"When are you going to learn a new word?" Natalie said. Disdain dripped from her voice.

Eve couldn't help laughing. Natalie had recently begun to act as if she were years older than her brother instead of just ten minutes. She tended to roll her eyes when he exaggerated or got too excited. She gave a lot of long-suffering sighs. And yet there were times when Nathan adopted the role of protector and Natalie actually allowed him to.

They were growing up, Eve reflected. Her heart ached as she thought about everything Adam had missed over the years. And if he ever *did* find out the truth about them, would he understand? Or would he hate her?

It's crazy to even consider seeing him again. The secret you kept from him is too huge for him to ever forgive you. He will *hate you, and then what? You'll be worse off than you were to begin with. And what if he decides to sue for visitation rights? Or even partial custody of the twins? Dear God. He wouldn't do that, would he?*

Oh, why had he come back? Maybe her life had been boring, but at least it had been peaceful. The twins had been safe. Eve's secret had been safe.

Now nothing was safe.

And yet, despite all the danger, despite her fear of what might happen, despite everything, she couldn't just walk away.

She wanted to see him again.

Eve couldn't face another evening at home alone. When she was alone, she tended to think too much. So when she finished the work she had to do at the office, she decided to drive to the San Marcos Outlets and do some shopping. If she was going to fly out to LA for a weekend, she needed some new clothes anyway.

She spent a pleasurable three hours browsing through Ann Taylor Factory Store, Banana Republic, Chico's and Kate Spade. She ended up with a new bikini and cover-up, a gorgeous print sundress, a couple of casual shirts and shorts, a pale blue summer sweater and a pair of metallic sandals. She ate a hot dog for her dinner and ended the evening at Tory Burch. She hadn't intended to buy anything there, just salivate over the beautiful designs, but saw a simply irresistible navy-and-white maxi dress that she could actually afford. Deciding she deserved to indulge herself a little, she bought it before she could talk herself out of it. The dress simply screamed California.

Happy as only a woman can be after a successful shopping trip and lots of pretty new clothes to wear, she arrived home at nine to see a familiar red Porsche sitting in front of her house. Her heart skidded, and her throat went dry.

Adam was back.

She pulled into the driveway and pressed the garage door opener, then pulled into the garage. By the time she got out of the car and retrieved her packages from the back, he had walked up behind her.

"Somebody's been shopping," he said.

Telling herself to be cool, she said, "Brilliant deduction, Sherlock."

He grinned. "Let me help you carry some of that."

For one second, she thought about refusing, then handed him the heaviest bags. Why refuse? She wanted him to come inside. No sense pretending otherwise.

She snapped on lights as they entered the house through the utility room. Glad she'd tidied over the weekend, she led the way into the kitchen, dropping her purse and bags on the kitchen table. He followed suit. Thinking fast, Eve headed straight to the fridge. "Would you like a beer? Or something else to drink?"

"A beer sounds good." He leaned against the countertop next to the sink. She couldn't help but notice how his jeans molded to his legs.

She took a bottle of Dos Equis out of the fridge and handed it to him. "This okay?"

His eyes met hers. "More than okay."

"There's an opener in the top drawer behind you." She reached for the half-full bottle of pinot grigio she kept chilled, then changed her mind and took out a can of Diet Coke instead. Maybe she'd best keep her wits about her tonight. She seemed to lose them anytime she was in proximity to Adam. "When did you get back?" she said as she took a glass out of the cupboard, added some ice, then poured in the contents of the can.

"This afternoon."

After taking a long swallow, she put her glass on the counter. "I'll just take my packages into the bedroom. Have a seat. I'll be right back."

Thankfully, he didn't suggest helping. Good thing, because the last place she wanted him was her bedroom. Not with *her* fast-disappearing willpower. After depositing the bags on her bed, she rejoined him in the kitchen. He was already seated at the table.

"You hungry?" she asked. "I've got some chips and salsa."

He shook his head. "I grabbed a burger earlier."

"So how did things go in Nashville?"

"Overall, pretty good. My bandmates were ecstatic to get some time off."

Every time he smiled at her, her heart squeezed. Why did he have to be so gorgeous? Not to mention sexy. And why did that smile of his constantly remind her how very careful she had to be to navigate these tricky waters?

"What about you?" he said, still smiling. "Do you have any vacation time coming?"

The question so startled her, she stammered when she answered. "Wh-why do you ask?"

"Because I was thinking maybe you'd like to go to Austin with me. Spend a few days. I need to check out the studio we're gonna be using, and I'd kind of like to check out the Sixth Street scene, too. And since your kids are gone and you're free…" He let the sentence drift off as he watched her reaction.

Eve drank some of her Diet Coke to give her time to think. Now her heart was going way too fast. Go to Austin with him? Even the thought of a few days away, just the two of them, was enough to make her feel weak in the knees. Good thing she was sitting down. "I, um, I don't know."

His smile faded, but his eyes held hers intently. "What don't you know, Eve?"

She took a deep breath. Told herself not to react like a child. *Be honest with him.* "I'm not sure it's a good idea for us to see each other anymore, Adam."

"You're not sure."

"No."

"You want to, though."

"Yes." *God help me, I do.*

"What are you afraid of?"

If only she could tell him. She sighed. "The truth?"

"Of course, the truth."

"I'm afraid I'll just get hurt." *Again.*

His eyes pinned hers. "Because I'm the kind of guy who hurts women?"

"That's not what I meant."

"What *did* you mean?"

"You know, Adam, we've already covered this ground. Your life is not here. Mine is. That spells trouble."

"My life doesn't *have* to be somewhere else, Eve."

He wasn't going to make this easy for her, was he?

"Look, Eve," he continued, "I just want to spend time with you while I'm here. I understand you're not sure. Hell, I'm not, either. We're just getting reacquainted, so it's too soon to know if this is going anywhere. But in the meantime, can't we be friends?"

"Friends," she said weakly. Friends with him? Was that even possible?

"How about this? We won't do anything you don't want to do. If our relationship progresses past simple friendship, it'll be because you want it to. Because you made the first move."

Dear Lord. What should she do? Everything in her was telling her even this much was a bad idea, but it was so tempting to say yes. She hadn't felt anything like this in such a long time. To go away with him, to spend a few days alone with him in a city where no one knew her, it was as if he were offering her the moon.

"It'll be fun. You'll relax and have a good time, I promise." When she still hesitated, he added, "You can trust me."

"Can I?" *Don't do it. It's a very bad idea. Tell him no. Tell him to go away.* "O-okay, I'll go."

He grinned. "Great! Let's go this weekend. Monday's the fourth, so that'll work out perfectly. If you take Friday off, we can leave Thursday when you're finished with work."

Much later, after he'd gone and Eve had put away all her new clothes and was getting ready for bed, she knew she could pretty much guarantee she'd be sorry she'd said yes to him. But right then, all she could think was how much she was looking forward to the weekend.

And all the possibilities it held.

On Wednesday, after visiting his mother, Adam and Austin had a meeting to discuss the contract Adam's agent had negotiated with the television network wanting him to star in his own series. Afterward, Austin said, "I've heard some rumors that Bethany may stir up some trouble for you."

Adam frowned. "How?"

"Word is she hired some private dick to do some digging."

"What!"

"Yeah, I know."

"What sort of digging?"

"Into your past, I guess. I don't know. She's pissed."

Adam sighed heavily. "I should have fired her."

"Then, she'd be even more pissed." Austin stared at him. "What you should have done was not get involved with her in the first place."

"I know. You don't have to rub it in."

"I just hope you've learned your lesson."

Adam nodded tiredly. "So what do you think I should do about this PI she's hired?"

"I don't think there's anything you *can* do. Let's see what happens. There's nothing for her to find that could be damaging, is there? You don't have a bunch of baby mamas hidden away, do you?"

"No! Of course not."

"No bodies buried in the backyard or anything."

Adam snorted with disbelief. "No."

"And you don't do drugs?"

"You know I don't."

"And you haven't plagiarized anyone else's music."

"I hope not."

"Okay, then…nothing to worry about."

Maybe there wasn't, but Adam didn't like any part of this. He decided he would be especially careful about the weekend. Although he didn't want to alarm Eve or give her any reason to back out of going to Austin with him, he knew he'd have to warn her about their keeping a low profile, though.

As it turned out, Eve was the one who introduced the subject. Adam called her on Wednesday, and before he could even suggest exercising caution, she said, "I was thinking, maybe it would be better for us to meet somewhere instead of you coming here and picking me up tomorrow night. My neighbors can be nosy."

"Good idea," he said. "No sense giving the gossips something to talk about."

"I'll drive over to the mall and park in the garage next to Dillard's. It'll be safe to leave my car there a few days."

"Will six o'clock work for you?"

"Perfect."

Eve didn't even have to call Adam when she arrived at the parking garage. She saw the red Porsche in the surface lot, and when she pulled into the garage, he was right behind her. She drove up to the second level where there was a crosswalk to the stores and parked where there were several empty spaces. By the time she'd cut her ignition and gotten out of the car, he was already opening the back of her Prius and taking out her suitcase. She locked the car and a few minutes later, they were on their way.

"Have you had dinner yet?" he asked once they were on the road.

"No, I wasn't hungry."

"We'll stop somewhere, then." He smiled at her. "I'm glad you're here."

"Me, too." And she really was, although she'd felt guilty when Bill had asked her if she wanted to come out to LA this weekend. She'd simply said she had plans, but either of the next two weekends would be great. He hadn't questioned her further, and for that she was grateful. She would have hated to lie to him.

He would be very upset when he found out. And she had no doubt he *would* eventually find out. Something like this was going to be impossible to keep secret forever.

It's not that big a deal. It's just this one weekend.

Eve sighed.

"What's wrong?"

"What do you mean, what's wrong?"

"You just sighed."

Eve laughed. "You heard that?"

"I hear everything."

"Nothing's wrong."

"C'mon, Eve. I know you better than that. What're you worried about?"

She shrugged. Looked at the passing countryside. Then she sighed again. "I was just thinking about Bill and how upset he'll be when he finds out what I was doing this weekend."

"It's none of his business, is it?"

"Not technically, but…he knows about you."

"About our past, you mean?"

"Yes."

"So what? Didn't he have other relationships before you?"

"I don't know."

"He knows about us, but you never asked about him?"

"He…he told me he'd been in love with me for years."

"So he was, what? Twenty-two or -three when you married him?"

"Yes."

"And he was a virgin?"

Adam sounded so skeptical, Eve had to bite back

a smile. "I don't know. Like I said, I didn't ask." But she *had* wondered.

"You must be the only woman in the world who isn't curious," Adam said.

Eve wondered what Adam would think if she told him the truth, that she hadn't cared enough to ask. But of course, she couldn't say that. Instead, she decided it was time to change the subject. "Where are we staying when we get to Austin?"

"Marty rented an apartment for me to use when I'm there. It's actually a furnished condo, and it's near the studio."

Eve was glad. She'd been concerned about walking into a hotel with Adam, imagining the repercussions if they happened to be photographed. She shuddered, just thinking about the tabloid headlines.

It didn't take long for them to reach the city limits, and once they did, Adam asked her if she was ready to eat.

"I'm still not very hungry."

"I'm not, either. We can go to the apartment first, unload our stuff, then see what's within walking distance. How does that sound?"

"Great."

Eve loved the apartment Adam's manager had found. A large two-bedroom condo, it was on the tenth floor of a co-op building and had a shaded balcony that gave them a view of downtown Austin. There was a security guard in the entry—which could only be accessed with a key card—elevators and an underground garage.

"This is really nice," she said.

Adam ceremoniously ushered her into the guest

bedroom. His eyes twinkled mischievously, and she couldn't help grinning back.

"Want to unpack before we take off?" he asked.

"Might as well. It'll only take a few minutes."

"Okay. I'll do the same."

Ten minutes later, her few garments hung in the closet, and the rest neatly tucked into a drawer, Eve joined Adam in the living room. And ten minutes after that, they discovered a small Italian restaurant a block away from the condo.

"What do you think?" Adam said.

"It looks good," Eve said after studying the menu posted outside.

It *was* good. Adam ordered the fettucine Bolognese and Eve ordered a mushroom ravioli dish that the owner assured her she would love. The restaurant was small enough to feel cozy and only half-full. No one paid the slightest attention to them, which made Eve relax and thoroughly enjoy both Adam's company and the excellent food and wine.

"That's the best meal I've had since your mother's pierogies," Adam said, patting his stomach. "I'm stuffed."

"Me, too," Eve said, "and it was delicious."

After Adam paid the bill, they walked out into the still-warm night. In the near distance they could hear music.

"Want to walk a bit?" Adam asked.

Eve nodded.

He offered his arm, and Eve tucked her hand under it. Even this casual contact made her breath catch. She wondered if he had any idea how he affected her. They strolled in the direction of the music, and Eve thought how right it seemed to be with him, to walk like this as if they were just an ordinary couple and not two people from opposite worlds who were forever separated by an enormous deception.

The music got louder as they approached the next block. It was coming from a small club with an open door from which several people emerged, talking and laughing.

"Want to go in?" Adam asked.

The music sounded inviting, a cross between swing and bluegrass. Still, Eve hesitated. What if someone inside recognized Adam? Did she want to take that chance? Her indecision must have shown on her face, because Adam quickly said, "We don't have to if you don't want to."

"No, let's go in."

"You sure?"

She smiled. "Yes."

Inside, they were seated at a small table in the back—the place was crowded—and their chairs were so close together that it was only natural for Adam to drape an arm behind her. Eve nearly stopped breathing, and everything in her went still. She was awash in sensations: the music pulsing around them, the beat of her heart, the musky scent of Adam's cologne, the warmth of his body next to hers, and underlying everything the desire throbbing deep within, a need so insistent she couldn't stop herself from turning to Adam.

His eyes met hers. In one long look a question was asked—and answered.

Tonight they would make love.

Chapter Ten

The walk back to the condo seemed to take forever. The ride up to the tenth floor was made in tense silence, with neither of them looking at each other. All Eve could think about was the moment when they would be alone.

The instant the door to the condo shut behind them, Eve was in Adam's arms. The kiss was hard and hungry, wet and demanding. They couldn't seem to get close enough, and he pushed her against the back of the door and ground himself against her.

This was not going to be a sweet, slow buildup of desire. What they were feeling had been too long in the making, too long in the waiting, too long in the wanting.

"I can't wait, Eve," he said.

And she could feel the truth of that, feel his heat against her.

"Take me," she cried.

With a moan, he lifted her into his arms and carried her into the master bedroom. Setting her on the bed, he unzipped his jeans while she removed her panties.

Pushing her dress up, he spread her legs apart and plunged into her. She was more than ready for him and wrapped her legs around him to give him better access.

"Eve!" he cried as he gave two more hard thrusts, then spilled his seed deep inside her.

She moaned and dug her nails into his back as she was racked with spasms.

They continued to move together until their passion was spent, then he collapsed against her. When their breathing finally calmed, he lifted himself and looked down at her.

"I'm sorry," he whispered. "I wanted our first time to be better. I wanted to give you more pleasure."

"But it's not our first time," she said softly, smiling up at him. He was so dear to her. She had missed him for such a long time.

"It feels like it," he said. He rolled off her, cradling her in his arms. He kissed the tip of her nose, then her mouth. His right hand cupped her breast, his thumb brushing its nub.

Eve closed her eyes.

"Do you like that?" he said, increasing the pressure.

"Y-yes."

"Let's take off these clothes." His voice sounded rough.

Minutes later, they lay entwined on the cool sheets, all the bedcovers tangled together with their clothes on the floor.

"You're so beautiful," he said as he stroked her body,

then followed with kisses. When his fingers found her sweet spot, moving in slow circles, she arched her back and gasped.

"Do you like that?" he said. His fingers stilled.

"Don't stop!" she cried.

He smiled. "I know how to make it even better." He pulled her against him spoon fashion, his left hand holding her breast, his right hand returning to the place crying out for his attention. She could feel his penis against her bottom, its heat pressing against her. She could feel herself climbing, climbing, and knew that when she reached the peak she would explode into a thousand pieces. His hand moved faster, and she couldn't hold back any longer. Her body convulsed, pleasure that was almost pain washing over her in furious waves.

He waited until her body had quieted, then lifted her up and set her on top of him. This time when he entered her, she felt every inch of him going deeper and deeper. And even though she couldn't have imagined climaxing again, desire built almost immediately, and this time, when he shuddered and jerked under her, she cried out with the force of another orgasm that didn't seem to want to end.

They slept after that. He pulled the sheet up, and she slept in his arms. When she finally awakened, she saw by the digital clock on the nightstand that it was four in the morning.

"You're awake," he murmured, kissing her neck.

"Um." She stretched. Her body didn't feel like her own.

"Last night was…amazing," he said, turning her toward him. He smiled, searching her eyes.

"Yes. It was." God, she loved his eyes.

"I'm only sorry about one thing."

"What?"

"I should have used a condom. But—"

"I know. We couldn't wait." She refused to think about the last time they'd made love and didn't use a condom.

"I'm clean, though. You know that, don't you? I would never endanger you—or anyone—in that way."

"I know." And she did. Adam was an honorable man. He always had been. She just hadn't given him a chance to prove it. But there was always the chance of a pregnancy. She opened her mouth to say so, then changed her mind. Best to stay away from the subject of unplanned pregnancies.

"Next time I'll make sure I have a condom."

"Next time?"

This time his smile was teasing. "There *will* be a next time, won't there? After all, we still have four days here."

She grinned. "Next time you're going to have to woo me. No more of this grabbing and throwing me on the bed."

He laughed. "You don't like caveman style, huh?"

"I didn't say that. But variety is the spice of life."

"Got it. Next time you will be suitably wooed."

Adam left Eve sleeping and had a long shower. Then he went into the kitchen and inspected the contents of the fridge. Good old Marty. He'd thoughtfully filled the fridge with orange juice, butter, eggs, bacon, milk, half-and-half, strawberry jam and a wedge of cheddar cheese. The vegetable keeper yielded tomatoes, green onions, mushrooms and red and yellow peppers. And the pantry contained a loaf of sourdough bread and plenty of coffee, as well as salt, black pepper, red pepper and sugar.

Adam wasn't a great cook, but he could manage breakfast. Since everything he needed for omelets was there, he decided he would surprise Eve and have one ready for her when she woke up.

When he heard her stirring, he put some butter in the frying pan he found and started getting his omelet ready. By the time she entered the kitchen, looking pretty doggone sexy in a short blue satin robe, he had the table set and the omelets ready.

"Good morning, gorgeous," he said. "All I have to do is butter the toast and we can eat."

"A man of many talents," she said, walking straight over to the coffeemaker and pouring herself a cup. She added half-and-half and a teaspoon of sugar.

He couldn't resist kissing her, and she felt so good in his arms, he almost wished he hadn't made breakfast yet so they could start the day with sex and follow up with food.

"Enough of that," she said, pushing him away when he would have kept kissing her. "I'm hungry."

"If I feed you first, can we have some fun afterward?"

She grinned. "So this is your idea of wooing? Cooking me breakfast?"

He'd forgotten about their agreement. But her reminder gave him an idea. "No, it's not. And you're right. I promised you some serious wooing, didn't I?"

"You did."

"Then, you shall have it."

So after they'd eaten and he'd shooed her off to take a shower while he cleaned up the kitchen, he made his plan. When he heard the shower go off and knew she was back in the bedroom, he tapped on the door. "Can I come in?"

"Might as well," she said. "After all, you've seen me naked."

Man, she looked good. He saw that she'd laid out a print sundress and had already put on a lacy yellow bra and matching bikini panties. "I'm going to leave you here by yourself for an hour or so, okay?"

She frowned. "Where are you going?"

"I have a couple of errands to run."

"Can't I go with you?"

"No."

"No? Just no? You're not going to give me a reason?"

"Let's just say my errands have to do with serious wooing."

Now she smiled. "In that case…" Walking over, she put her arms around him and lifted her face for his kiss.

Twenty minutes later, with Eve happily ensconced on the balcony with a fresh cup of coffee and his promise that he'd back in less than an hour and a half, he was on his way to take care of his first errand.

True to his word, and extremely pleased with himself, he returned to the condo a little before noon. Putting his purchases in the safe and ignoring Eve's curious look, he said, "I'd like to go look at the studio, then we can grab some lunch somewhere. How does that sound?"

"Great," she said.

They walked to the studio, which was only three blocks away. It turned out to be perfect, but he'd expected that. Marty wasn't his manager for nothing. After Adam had inspected everything, they headed out to find a place to eat. This time they settled on a seafood restaurant that specialized in Cajun food, which happened to be one of Adam's favorites. Over bowls of gumbo they talked about Adam's plans for the future.

"Once the tour is over, I'd like to just concentrate on writing new music," he said.

"In Nashville?"

"I'd probably divide my time between there and LA."

"Really? You like California?"

"I do. And so do my bandmates."

"You have a house there?"

"In Malibu."

"You really have the perfect life, don't you?"

The question wasn't coy. So he gave it a thoughtful answer. "It lacks one thing to make it perfect." When she didn't bite and ask what that might be, he plunged ahead. "Someone to share that life with."

She met his gaze squarely. "Yes. I understand that."

He wanted to say more. But it was too soon. There were too many things unsettled between them. He hadn't even met her children yet. So he remained quiet, and so did she.

After lunch, he suggested finding a bookstore where they could get a few books, and maybe some games and puzzles. "We'll go out tonight, but I thought you might enjoy a relaxing afternoon."

"I like that idea," she said.

An hour later, loaded down with not only books, a couple of games and puzzles, but also several DVDs, a couple of bottles of wine and snacks, they headed back to the condo.

Eve fell asleep over her book, and Adam let her sleep. He enjoyed watching her and thought how pleasant it was to share a quiet afternoon with no phone calls and nothing pressing to do—just the anticipation of another evening with Eve, one where he could begin the serious wooing he'd promised her. He smiled, remembering the treasures he'd put in the safe. He couldn't wait to see her face when he gave her the first of the surprises he'd planned. In fact, maybe he'd go get it now. Put it on the table next to her so she'd see it when she woke up.

He was glad he'd asked the owner of the shop where he'd purchased the gifts to wrap them, because the flat velvet box looked prettier in the silver paper and matching bow than it would have looked unadorned.

Now all he had to do was wait.

Eve sighed in her sleep. She knew she was dreaming, but it was such a lovely dream she didn't want it to end. In it, she and Adam and the twins were having a picnic. It was a beautiful summer's day, and they'd spread a big quilt out next to the river—she recognized the river, it was the one running through Crandall Lake. They'd finished eating and now the twins were dangling their bare feet in the water while she and Adam lay on the quilt watching them.

They were so happy, all of them. Adam loved the twins and they loved him. They had a perfect life, just the four of them. How this perfection had come about, Eve didn't know, and she didn't care. They were together. That was all that mattered.

"Hey, sleepyhead."

Eve frowned. She closed her eyes tighter.

"It's time to get up. It's almost five o'clock."

Reluctantly, she opened her eyes to see Adam smiling down at her. "Five o'clock?" she said. "Really?"

"Really. You slept more than two hours."

She stretched and yawned, then rubbed her eyes. Darn, she hated to let go of her dream. "So what's the plan?"

"Well, first you're going to open your present. After that, we'll decide what we want to do."

"My present?"

"It's right there." Adam inclined his head toward the end table next to her chair.

Eve's eyes widened as she saw the beautifully wrapped box. "That's for *me*?"

"Yes, it's for you."

"It's not my birthday."

"I know that. But it is a serious wooing day."

She laughed, delighted.

"Open it," Adam said eagerly.

She carefully removed the silvery paper, and when she saw the gray velvet box, her heart began to beat faster. Almost afraid to open it, she hesitated.

"It won't bite. Open it!" Adam said.

"Oh," she said as she saw the gorgeous strand of graduated pearls nestled inside the satin interior. The diamond clasp winked under the afternoon sunlight.

"As soon as I saw these I knew they'd look perfect on you," Adam said softly. He lifted them out of the box and walked around behind her. "Let me put them on you."

"I—I don't know what to say." The pearls were way

too expensive. She knew that. She hoped he didn't think she was hinting that she wanted jewelry when she'd said she wanted to be wooed. Because that wasn't what she'd meant at all.

Adam fastened them around her neck, then reached for her hand and brought her to her feet. "Go look in the mirror. They look beautiful on you."

They *were* beautiful. Eve could hardly believe *how* beautiful.

"Do you like them?"

"Like them? I *love* them, but, Adam, I—I'm not sure I can accept them."

"Of course you can. They were made for you. *You* were made for beautiful jewelry. And I have something else to go with them." He reached into his pocket and took out a small box, also wrapped in silver paper.

Her hands were shaking as she unwrapped the second box. She was terrified that inside she'd find an engagement ring. Surely not. Surely he wouldn't just spring something like that on her, would he? But it wasn't a ring inside. Instead, there was a pair of exquisite diamond earrings. "Adam, this is too much. I can't take these."

"Well, I'm not taking them back. And they'll look a heck of lot better on you than they would on me."

"I didn't mean for you to buy me things when I said—"

"I know you didn't. I wanted to. I want to buy you everything, Eve. Everything you've never had. Everything you've ever wanted."

All I want is you. And I'm afraid that's something I'll never be able to have.

Some of what she was thinking must have shown in her eyes, because Adam's eyes softened and he reached for her. "You deserve these, Eve. Don't spoil the pleasure it gives me to give them to you. Just wear them and enjoy them, okay?" He kissed her then, slowly and sweetly, and when he said, "Why don't we shower together while we get ready for the evening?" she didn't have to be asked twice.

Eve had never showered with Bill. He'd suggested it once, but she'd begged off with some excuse and he hadn't pushed her. Showering with Adam was a revelation. After last night, she hadn't imagined she could be any more turned on by lovemaking than she had been already, but she'd been wrong. There was something so erotic and sensuous and almost wanton about the sensation of the hot water cascading over them as Adam simultaneously soaped her and explored her body that it elicited responses she hadn't known she was capable of making. She clung to Adam, weak and trembling and satiated, after another powerful orgasm shuddered through her.

Afterward, he tenderly dried her and smoothed lotion onto her body. "Now me," he said.

She happily obliged, enjoying the ripple of his muscles as she massaged in the lotion. She gave special attention to the insides of his thighs, especially when she saw his reaction. "Not again!" she said, laughing. "I can't."

"I didn't think I could, either," he said ruefully. "But as you see…"

"It'll just have to wait until later." When he would have caught her to try to persuade her otherwise, she managed to dart away.

"Oh, okay," he said, pretending to be angry.

After she'd put on her undergarments and was looking through the clothes she brought to decide what to wear, he said, "How about the black dress? We'll go somewhere fancy."

"Are you getting dressed up, too?"

"I'll wear a suit."

"Really?" For some reason, this delighted her.

"For you, sweet cheeks, anything."

Later, as they enjoyed excellent steaks at Sullivan's, which had been recommended to Adam, Eve thought how she could get used to this life. But that was dangerous thinking. Because no matter how she wrapped her mind around it, she couldn't come up with a solution to her problem. She had kept something important from Adam, something that would have changed his life had he known about it, and if he ever discovered what it was, he would no longer have any desire to be with her. He would probably despise her and never want to see her again.

"What's wrong?"

Eve started. "Nothing's wrong. Why do you ask?" She attempted a smile, but knew it wasn't very successful.

"You looked awfully serious. Are you okay?"

"I'm fine."

"You sure?"

"I'm sure." He was so thoughtful. She thought about the beautiful pearls, and the diamond earrings, both of which she was wearing tonight. No one had ever pampered her like this. If only she could be totally honest with him.

"There's that frown again. Something's bothering you, Eve. I wish you'd tell me what it is."

Eve sighed. She'd have to say something. "I guess I'm worried that someone is going to recognize you… and Bill is going to find out where I am. I should have told him."

"Why do you feel so obligated? Hell, he remarried, didn't he?"

"Yes."

"Does he tell you what he's doing every minute of the day? And who he's with?"

"No."

"Then, I don't get it. You don't owe him an explanation."

But I do. And if you knew why, you'd hate me. "I'm sorry. I'm being silly. Let's not talk about this anymore, okay? I don't want to spoil our evening."

He started to say something else, then stopped. "No, I'm the one who's sorry. You're not being silly. There's always a chance we'll be spotted by the paparazzi and you'll see yourself on the cover of one of the tabloids. So far they've been leaving me alone, mainly because Aaron spends a lot of time on Twitter and Instagram and that keeps fans thinking they know what I'm doing." He frowned. "I hate that part of my life, Eve. All I really want to do is write music."

"But you like performing, too."

"Yeah, but I don't like all the crap that comes with it."

Eve nodded, glad he was no longer worrying about her. She finished her steak and sank back in her chair, replete. "That was a wonderful meal, Adam. Thank you."

He reached across the table and took her hand. "You're welcome." Their gazes met. "But the best is yet to come."

When he looked at her like that, she felt it all the way down to her toes. The promise in his eyes made her heart skitter, and suddenly she didn't care whether they went club hopping or did anything else. All she wanted was to go back to the condo and spend the rest of the weekend in that lovely king-size bed of his. Since these weeks while the twins were away would probably be the last time she'd ever have with Adam, she wanted to make the most of them and store up as many memories as possible. "Does that mean what I think it means?" she said softly.

"It can mean whatever you want."

"Then, let's go back to the condo."

His smile was all the answer she needed.

The rest of the weekend was spent making love. In bed, out of bed, in the shower, standing up, lying down. They couldn't seem to get enough of each other. And in between the really amazing sex, they ate and slept and cuddled on the couch and occasionally got dressed and went out for a long walk. They never did hit the music scene on Sixth Street, but neither of them cared.

The idyllic weekend couldn't last forever, though. Too soon it was Monday and time to head home again. Eve was just thankful that no one had spied them in Austin and that no photographs had been taken. At least now she wouldn't have to worry about upsetting Bill or having a confrontation she wasn't ready for.

She felt sad as they prepared to leave. She would never forget this place. Never forget this weekend. Although no promises had been made and no words of love had been spoken, she'd never felt so treasured— and yes, loved. Adam had shown her, in every possible way, that she was important to him, and that he wanted nothing except for her to be happy.

She wished she could tell him how she felt and how much this time away with him had meant to her. But she couldn't. She was just grateful to have had these wonderful days and nights. When she was a very old woman she would take out these memories like old photographs, and they would remind her she'd once been deeply loved.

"You're awfully quiet," he said as they looked around the condo, making sure they hadn't forgotten anything.

"I'm sad to leave," she admitted.

"We'll do it again."

She smiled, but inside she was thinking, *No, we won't. Soon all of this will be over and you'll go back to your real life.*

The drive back to Crandall Lake went far too fast. By the time they reached the mall and the garage where she'd left her car, tears were clogging her throat.

Adam took her bag out of his car and put it in the back of hers. Then, since no one was around to see, he pulled her close and gave her a long, lingering kiss. "Thank you for the weekend," he whispered as he released her. "I'll call you tomorrow."

She nodded.

He waited until she was in her car before getting back into his. Then, with a smile and a wave, he drove away. When he rounded the corner and was out of sight, she finally let go, putting her head down on the steering wheel and letting the tears come.

Chapter Eleven

"Mom, we went to the San Diego Zoo yesterday! It was so cool! You should have seen all the flamingos!"

Eve couldn't help smiling at the exuberance in Natalie's voice. She'd known they were going to the zoo. She'd talked to the twins every day since they'd left. That was the beauty of cell phones. You could be in Alaska or Russia and no one would know the difference, so they'd had no idea she wasn't at home the past few days. And being kids, they hadn't been curious about what she was doing anyway. They were too full of what they were doing.

"When are you going to come out here and visit?" Natalie was asking now. "Dad said maybe this weekend?"

"Yes. I'll be there Friday." It would be good for her to get away. Very soon, she would once again have to get used to a life without Adam, and this would be good practice. "Now let me talk to Nathan."

Later, after they'd hung up, Eve's thoughts returned to Adam. He had texted her this morning, suggesting they go for a drive when she finished work today. If she had any brains, she'd beg off. Say she was tired or had to work tonight—or something.

"You won't do that, though," Olivia had said earlier when they'd talked.

Eve had sighed. "No, probably not."

And she hadn't. When Adam called her late in the afternoon, she said she'd be ready by six. She told him she'd leave her car in the newspaper parking lot, so he could pick her up there.

At six, when she emerged into the hot afternoon sun, he was again waiting for her by leaning against his car. When he saw her, he straightened, grinned and opened the passenger door. And even though they were normally discreet, he couldn't seem to resist dropping a quick kiss on her mouth before helping her into the car.

Eve heard the telltale click of the camera before she saw the dark young man across the street. Oh, God. Someone had taken a picture of her and Adam, probably when he'd kissed her. The man was continuing to take pictures as Adam walked around and got into the car with her.

"Damn bloodsuckers," Adam muttered. He gunned the motor and they took off down the street.

Eve's heart was pounding. Where would those photos end up? And would Bill see them? Why had she let Adam kiss her? She knew better.

"I'm sorry, Eve," Adam said as they headed for the highway. "I guess I got complacent. The newspeople have left me alone since I've been here, and I guess I thought they'd continue to."

"What do you think they'll do with those pictures?"

Adam shrugged. "I don't know. Maybe they'll just show up online."

"Instead of the tabloids, you mean?"

"Yeah."

Eve guessed all she could do was pray that was the case. *And* that the photographer didn't know who she was. Because if her name was published along with a picture of Adam kissing her, a phone call from Bill was going to be the least of her problems.

"I guess your promises don't mean much."

Eve closed her eyes. Bill was furious, and she couldn't blame him. The photo of Adam kissing her had been splashed on the cover of *Star*, which graced every supermarket checkout line in the country. And the story accompanying the picture had made Eve cringe, suggesting she was the real reason Adam was spending so much time in his hometown. "What's the story between these old friends?" the article asked. "Is there more than meets the eye? Is blonde beauty Eve Kelly the real reason behind Adam Crenshaw's breakup with Bethany D'Angelo?"

Whoever had written the article had done his or her research, too, because they'd given a short biography of Eve, including the fact she had two children. Fortunately, their names and ages weren't included, and for that Eve was grateful. Still, she knew Bill had good reason to be upset and she also knew she deserved his anger.

"I'm sorry, Bill," she said after he'd finished his initial venting.

"I don't understand you, Eve. I thought we had a meeting of the minds."

"We did. We do. I just—"

"You just, what?"

"I wanted to spend some time with him before he leaves for good," she said quietly and with as much dignity as she could muster.

"And where does that leave me, Eve? Are you going to go back on your original promise, too?"

"No! Of course not. I—I wouldn't do that to you."

"I don't know how I can believe you."

"Bill…"

"Just tell me one thing. Are you in love with him?"

Eve bit her lip. How could she answer that question?

"That's what I thought," Bill said tiredly.

Neither spoke for a long moment. Finally Eve said, "Do you still want me to come out for the weekend?"

"Not if those damned photographers are going to follow you out here."

Eve's mouth dropped open. She'd never thought of that. "They…they wouldn't."

"You sure about that?"

"It's Adam they're interested in, not me." But her heart had sunk. What had she done?

"Maybe you should forget about coming out," Bill said. "I'll figure out something to tell the twins."

"Don't punish me for this, Bill. I want to see them. I'm coming. I—I'll stay at a hotel."

"I guess I can't stop you. But, Eve? Just make sure you come alone."

* * *

Adam was thoroughly pissed off by the picture splashed not only on the cover of *Star*, but repeated again and again on Twitter, Facebook, Instagram and Tumblr, then picked up by *People*, *In Touch* and *Us Weekly*. In the space of twenty-four hours, it seemed every gossip rag in the country had latched on to his relationship with Eve, calling her the "mystery woman" from his past and the "forbidden love" he'd been hiding by pretending his mother's health was the only reason he'd continued to stay in Crandall Lake. *Entertainment Tonight* even did a story on his life before he became famous and speculated that Eve might be "the girl he left behind," might even be the girl he'd been thinking of when he wrote "Impossible to Forget." That this was true didn't help his mood.

It wasn't that he minded personally if people knew about Eve. But he knew how she felt. She *did* mind, because she had two children to consider. It would be one thing if the two of them were really a couple and committed to one another, but that wasn't the case— yet. And maybe it never would be, especially if the paparazzi started hounding them. They might scare Eve off permanently.

Adam was so fed up, he felt like decking someone. He could only imagine how Eve felt. He called her immediately after Austin had called to alert him about the photo, but the call had gone to voice mail. He wondered if she wasn't picking up because she was busy or because she didn't want to talk to him. He wouldn't blame her if the latter were true. He kept trying to reach her all afternoon with no success, so he drove over to the newspaper office, but her car wasn't in the parking lot. He finally resorted to calling on her mother.

"Come on in, Adam," her mother said when she opened the door.

"I'm looking for Eve," he said, "and thought maybe you'd know where she is."

"She went to San Antonio today to interview Kelly Simonson. You know, she's the one running for the open state senate seat in November."

"Oh." So Eve wasn't trying to evade him. "Well, I'm sorry to have bothered you. I was just worried she was upset."

"About that picture?"

"Yes."

Anna nodded sympathetically. "Why don't you come in and sit down? I'll give you something to drink, and we can talk. You look as if you need a shoulder."

Once Adam was settled in the living room with a glass of iced tea and Anna sitting across from him, she said, "That picture of the two of you is the talk of the town."

He sighed heavily. "Yeah."

"Eve is definitely upset."

"I figured. I wanted to apologize."

"Why? It's not your fault it happened."

"I should have been more careful."

"If you and Eve continue to see one another, something like this was bound to happen sooner or later, Adam. No matter how careful you are."

"Is that how Eve feels?"

"Well, not yet, but she will. She's an adult, Adam. She knew what she was getting into."

"Did she? No one really knows until they're in it. Hell, I didn't know what it was gonna be like."

"There's no privacy in public life."

"No, there's not."

"And if Eve's going to be a part of your life, she'll have to get used to that."

Adam stared at Eve's mother. She sounded as if she approved of his relationship with her daughter. His spirits lifted. If Eve's mother liked him, if she approved of him, maybe there really was a chance for him and Eve.

"*Is* Eve going to be a part of your life?" Anna asked after a long moment had gone by.

"I don't know," Adam answered honestly. "I'd like her to be, but she seems to think our lives are too different."

"They are different, but that's not necessarily a bad thing, is it?"

Adam smiled, feeling better by the minute.

Anna's blue eyes were warm with understanding. "I'll tell you what I think, Adam. I think if you love her and want her, you'll figure out a way to persuade her the two of you can make this work."

Eve finally answered Adam's messages by texting him late Tuesday, once she'd returned from San Antonio.

Too tired to talk tonight. I'll call U tomorrow.

He answered immediately.

OK. Been worried about U.

Eve sighed when she read his response. Their conversation tomorrow wasn't going to be easy.

And it wasn't. She was working at home, so she called him a little after nine. He answered immediately.

"Sorry about yesterday," she said. "I was bummed and just not in the mood to talk."

"I know. I wanted to strangle that photographer."

"He was just doing his job."

"Hell of a way to make a living."

"We should have been more careful."

"I know. I have to take the blame for it."

"It was my fault, too."

"When you didn't answer my calls yesterday, I thought you were mad at me."

Eve smiled tiredly. "I was mad at myself. Besides, what happened was inevitable."

"Eve, look. Let's table this discussion until we can see each—"

"No, Adam," she interrupted, "let me say what I have to say. I've booked a flight to LA for tomorrow. I'll be gone five days. I need to see my kids and talk to Bill…and kind of get my head straight on some things. Then, when I come back next Tuesday, you and I can talk. That is, if you still want to."

"If I still *want* to? What does that mean, Eve?"

She sighed heavily. "Just what I said. If you still want to."

"Of course I'll still want to. I want to now. The question is, will *you*?"

The weight of what lay between them had never seemed so insurmountable. "I don't know. You have to give me some time."

As if he finally accepted it would be impossible to

change her mind, he agreed with only token protests, and they ended the call with her promising to phone him the next night after she was settled into her hotel.

She dreamed about him that night. But it wasn't a happy dream, not like the one she'd had before where she and Adam and the twins were having that picnic. This dream was more like a nightmare, with Bill and Missy and little Will and the twins and Adam and her mother's nosy neighbor and the mayor of Crandall Lake and that photographer who'd taken their picture all in it together.

And the next morning, when Eve awakened, there were tears on her face, and she knew she'd been crying in her sleep.

Unfortunately, she was afraid there were a lot more tears in her future, because no matter how she looked at her situation, she simply could not see a happy ending.

Adam waited two days. Two days of pacing around, wondering what was happening in California, two days of unsatisfactory phone calls with Eve, two days of inaction.

He hated inaction.

He was a person who *acted.* He didn't believe in leaving his fate in someone else's hands.

So on Saturday he booked a first-class ticket to LA, told his brothers and his mother he'd be gone for a few days but would see them early next week, and then drove to the Austin airport.

Six hours later he landed at LAX. Unfortunately, someone had alerted the local paparazzi—probably tweeted from the plane—and camera shutters whirred around him as he exited the airport and saw his limo driver waiting for him. As the driver navigated the heavy traffic on the 405, Adam thought about where and how he should tackle the problem of Eve and her fears.

Maybe he should just call her ex. Talk to him frankly, man-to-man, to allay any fears Bill might have that Adam's relationship with Eve would disrupt their lives in negative ways.

But doing that might upset Eve even more.

And Adam couldn't afford to upset her any more than she was now.

Instead, he would have flowers delivered to her the next morning, with a card saying he was in the hotel restaurant and would she please join him. And if she didn't, if she ignored him, he would wait in the lobby until she emerged. She couldn't hide from him forever.

He had just ordered his breakfast and was drinking a cup of coffee when his phone buzzed.

You're here? In California?

Rather than texting her back, he called. "I'm sorry," he said when she answered, "but I couldn't just sit in Crandall Lake and do nothing. I had to come out. Please come down here and talk to me."

She finally agreed, but it took her an hour. He'd eaten his breakfast and had several cups of coffee before he saw her walk into the restaurant. His heart lifted. Although she looked way too serious, he could see the two days with her children had agreed with her. She looked beautiful and more relaxed, dressed in tapered white pants with a bright blue crop top and blue sandals. Her hair was pulled back in a ponytail and secured with a blue ribbon. She looked years younger than she actually was.

"This is not a good idea, Adam," she said once she was seated. She still hadn't smiled.

"I'm not good at waiting."

She didn't answer as their waiter handed her a menu, then poured her a cup of coffee. But when he walked away, she met Adam's gaze levelly. "I just don't know what you think coming here is going to accomplish."

Adam knew he had to go all in. There was no other reason for him to have taken this gamble. "I guess I hoped you were missing me as much as I was missing you." He lowered his voice so that she had to lean closer to hear him. "I've been missing you for too many years, Eve. Don't you think it's time we did something about that?"

To her credit, she didn't look away. "I just... Our lives are so different, Adam. I'm not free. You know that. I—I have two children. And you haven't...you haven't even met them yet."

"That's another reason I'm here. I want to meet them. Why don't you give them a call? Tell them you want to take them to Venice Beach today."

"What am I supposed to do? Lie to Bill?"

"No. I know you're not comfortable lying. So tell him the truth, that you're meeting me, that I want to meet your kids. Make it clear that I'm a part of your life now and he'll just have to get used to it."

Her face had flushed as he talked, and he could see how conflicted she was. For some reason, she was terrified. Her mother had been right. It was up to him to make Eve see her fears could be dealt with, that a future between them wasn't an impossibility, that whatever she imagined the obstacles to be, they could surmount them.

"I—I don't have a car," she said.

"That's not a problem. I'll call my driver and send you to Bill's in the limo. Luther will wait while you go in and collect your kids. We'll meet at the Ferris wheel at Santa Monica Pier."

She swallowed. "I don't know…"

"Don't make this such a big deal. We'll have a great time." What was she so afraid of? "Your kids know we're friends. Didn't you tell me your daughter was disappointed she hadn't met me yet?"

After a deep sigh, she finally said, "Okay."

Adam grinned. "Call Bill now."

"I'll go out to the lobby and do it while you take care of the bill."

Five minutes later, check paid and phone call to Luther made, he walked out to the lobby and saw her just finishing her phone call. "Everything okay?" he asked as he approached.

She nodded. "I didn't tell him yet."

"Why not?"

"I didn't want to do it over the phone. I'll tell him when I get there."

He nodded. "Do you think he's going to make a scene?"

She shrugged. "I don't know."

Adam squeezed her shoulder. "It'll be okay. Once you tell him, the worst will be over."

"Will it?" The worry in her eyes was still there.

"Look, if it'll make it easier for you, I'll go with you."

"No! That'll make it worse. I'll do it."

"All right. Whatever you say. Want to go outside to wait? Luther should be here any minute."

"Okay." She opened her purse and took out a pair of sunglasses.

When they walked outside, Adam saw there were several photographers gathered along the curb.

"Oh, God," Eve said.

"They're not here because of me," Adam said, taking her arm and leading her away. "That's one of the Kardashian girls over there." He put on his own sunglasses.

He was right. No one bothered them as they waited in front of the boutique next door. Eve kept biting her lip, and Adam wished he could think of something to make her relax, but he'd done all he could. So he said nothing and was grateful when he saw Luther pull up to the curb a few minutes later.

After helping her into the limo, he said, "It's all going to be fine, Eve."

"Is it?" Her eyes were hidden behind her dark glasses.

"Yes." He leaned over and kissed her briefly. "I'll see you soon." He wished he had the right to say he loved her, but that would have to wait. First he had to meet her children and win them over.

Then, and only then, would he be free to put all his cards on the table.

Chapter Twelve

Eve told Luther to park across the street from the cottage Bill and his family were living in rather than in front of it. She didn't want Adam's driver to hear what Bill had to say when he found out what she and Adam had planned.

Her stomach was jittery as she walked up the path to the front door. She hated confrontations, especially with Bill. She always seemed to come out the loser. *But that was preordained, wasn't it? From the moment you accepted his proposal of marriage, you agreed to his terms. You have no one but yourself to blame for any of it.*

"How'd you get here?" Bill asked when he opened the door.

"Where are the twins?" she countered.

"They went to the store with Missy." He was frowning, squinting against the bright sunlight reflected off the ocean beyond. "They'll be back any minute."

"Oh. Okay."

"So how did you get here?"

"Um, that car across the street."

"That *limo*, you mean?"

"Yes."

"You rented a *limo*?"

"Um, no. Um, can we go inside?"

"Oh, sure. Sorry. C'mon in."

As she walked into the small entry, she could see the baby in his playpen in the living area beyond. She smiled. He really was a doll. "Will's getting so big."

Bill smiled proudly. "He is, isn't he?" Leading the way into the living room, he invited her to sit down. "The kids'll be excited to ride in a limo."

"Yes." Eve took a deep breath. She had to tell him now, before Missy and the kids got back, before she lost her courage. "Bill, there's something I need to tell you. Adam is here, in LA. The limo is his. The kids and I are going to meet him at the Santa Monica Pier."

Bill stared at her. "What do you mean, he's here? Didn't we talk about this? Didn't you promise to come alone?"

"I didn't know he was coming. He just showed up. Came in late last night and didn't tell me until he was already at my hotel."

"Christ, Eve, he's not *staying* there?"

"No, no, he's not. He has a house in Malibu. He just…came to the restaurant this morning."

"You know, he has one helluva lot of nerve. If I were him, I wouldn't want to show my face in public today. But I guess his kind don't care how much gossip there is about them. Just as long as you get your name plastered all over the place."

"What are you talking about?"

"So he hasn't told you, huh?"

"Told me what?"

Bill got up, walked to a table near the front window and picked up a copy of the *Los Angeles Times.* He riffled through the pages, then shoved a section in front of her. At the top of the page, under the header News & Notes, there was a big picture of Adam and a beautiful redhead. The caption read, "Adam Crenshaw and his baby mama?" Eve's heart began to pound. The brief story said the woman pictured was Bethany D'Angelo, Adam's publicity manager and recent girlfriend, who had just announced she was pregnant with Adam's child. "He'd better not try to deny it," she'd told the reporter, "because the proof is right here." So saying, she'd patted her stomach and smiled. "He can't just walk away from this the way he's tried to walk away from me."

Eve felt sick.

"I don't want you taking the twins with you today," Bill said coldly. "I think you need to do some hard thinking, don't you? Is this the kind of thing you want them exposed to? First the tabloid stories about you and now the stories about this woman and their baby? What's next?"

"I—I didn't know," Eve whispered. Had Adam? He couldn't have. He would have told her, wouldn't he? Of course he would have. He wasn't a liar. *Not like you are.* "What will we tell the kids?"

"You won't tell them anything. You're going to go out and get in that limo and get out of here before they come back. I'll tell them you called and aren't feeling well. That you said to tell them you'll see them tomorrow when you're better."

Because Eve really did feel sick now, she didn't argue. Anyway, Bill was right. The kids didn't need to be there when she and Adam talked about this.

Luther looked at her quizzically when she got in the car and told him to take her to the Santa Monica Pier. Because he was obviously trained not to, he didn't question her about the whereabouts of her twins or why they weren't coming with them. He just pulled away from the curb and headed down the street.

Just before they turned the corner at the end of the block, she saw Missy and the twins approaching. Nathan was pulling a red wagon loaded with grocery bags, and Natalie was skipping ahead. They took no notice of the limo, but even if they had, the windows were tinted so dark they would not have seen Eve.

Tears rolled down Eve's face and she angrily wiped them away. She was sick to death of crying over Adam. Disappointment lodged in her belly, but along with the disappointment was gratitude. Because she'd been lucky. She'd found out the truth of what her life would be like if she spent the rest of it with Adam, and the discovery had come before she'd made the second biggest mistake of her life.

Now all that was left was for her to tell Adam it was over.

Adam watched the happy kids and the adults accompanying them as they rode the Ferris wheel. Soon he and Eve and her twins would be joining them. He was excited; he'd been wanting to meet Eve's children for a long time now. He was also nervous. He wanted them to like him. He knew they probably would; he was good with kids, plus he had the fame thing going. Although he hated to admit it, his fame could be a good thing instead of the noose around his neck he often complained about.

He stood at the railing at the edge of the pier and looked out over the ocean. The water sparkled as if a million diamonds had been sprinkled over it. He had to admit, as much as he loved Nashville, LA had a lot to recommend it. For one thing, people didn't bother him. They were so used to celebrities out here that they pretty much ignored him unless he was appearing at a performance.

And then there was the ocean, which was always magnificent, something he never tired of looking at. He couldn't wait to take Eve to his house in Malibu. He knew she'd love it with its ocean views and open, contemporary styling. The kids would love it there, too.

He looked at his watch. Luther had picked Eve up an hour ago. They should be coming to the pier any-time now. He decided to walk out to where the limo would have to stop, since it couldn't drive onto the pier.

Minutes later, he saw the car approaching, and his heart lifted. He was smiling when the limo stopped and Eve got out. The smile quickly faded when he re-alized she was alone.

"Where're the kids?" he said, walking toward her.

"They're not coming." She didn't smile.

Adam swore softly. He guessed her ex wasn't quite the nice guy she'd portrayed. "Should I have Luther wait?"

"That's up to you. There's something we need to discuss."

Now he frowned. What was the matter with her? She looked as if she were upset with *him*. What had changed since they'd parted at the hotel? Walking over to the car, he waited till Luther had lowered the driver's-side window, then said, "Why don't you go on home? I'll call you when I need you."

Luther nodded. "Okay, boss."

Once car and driver were gone, Adam said, "Let's walk, okay?" When they'd gone a far enough distance from the pier to have some privacy, he said, "What happened?"

"Have you read today's paper?"

"No. Why?"

"Your ex-girlfriend, Bethany, has made an accusation."

"About *me*?"

"Yes."

Austin was wrong. Adam *should* have fired her. "What'd she say?"

"That she's carrying your baby."

"What?"

"So you didn't know?"

"Hell, no, I didn't know." His mind whirled. Was it possible? He had always taken precautions with Bethany. Not just to prevent an unwanted pregnancy, but because he believed in safe sex, for his partner's protection as much as his own. How could Bethany be pregnant? Especially with *his* child? "That doesn't make any sense. We've never had unprotected sex."

"Birth control isn't foolproof," Eve said.

Adam didn't know what to say. Eve wouldn't meet

his eyes. He couldn't help thinking that she was re-membering how just a week ago he hadn't used a con-dom with her. Maybe she thought he was lying about using them with Bethany.

"Bill showed me the story," Eve finally said.

"That's why he didn't want you to bring the kids today."

Eve nodded, looking out over the water. She seemed a million miles away. "I don't blame him."

The way she was acting hurt. "I think it's interesting how I've been tried and convicted already. You seem to feel the same way Bill does."

Her head whipped around, and now her eyes were blazing. "How *should* I feel, Adam? Happy? Today only proved what I've been thinking for a long time. Any relationship with you means the entire world will know my business. My whole life will be spread out for people to judge."

So *that* was what her fear was all about. "Look, I can't deny that the tabloids love to leap on anything that smacks of scandal, but we wouldn't be living that kind of life. There'd be nothing interesting to write about, and they'd soon forget about us. Oh, hell, this is not the way I wanted to do this, but thanks to Bethany, it looks as if I no longer have a choice." He reached into his pocket, where he'd been carrying something around for a while now, waiting for the right moment. Extract-ing the small velvet box, he opened it to reveal a gor-geous Neil Lane diamond ring. "I bought this when we were in Austin, Eve. I love you. I've always loved you, and I want us to be together, to build a family together. That's why I was so eager to meet your kids today. I was hoping you'd say you'll marry me."

The color had drained from her face as he spoke.

"What do you say?" he asked gently. "Will you marry me?"

Her eyes filled with tears, and she shook her head. "I—I don't know what to say."

"Say you love me. Say yes."

"I can't."

"Why not? Is it Bill?" When she didn't answer, he said, "He can't stop you, you know."

"You don't understand."

"You're right. I don't." He reached for her hand, tried to put the box in it, but she wouldn't take it. "I never thought you were a coward, Eve. If you're afraid to tell him, I'll go with you. I'll tell him. We'll tell him together."

Her eyes widened, and now two bright spots of color blazed on her cheeks. "No! I... You have to give me some time. I—I can't... I can't give you an answer today. I have to think about all this."

Knowing he was beaten—at least for now—he sighed heavily, closed the box and put it back in his pocket. "Fine. You think about it, and I'll go back to Crandall Lake and talk to Austin about Bethany. Have him investigate and see if she's telling the truth."

"And if she is?"

"If she is and I *am* the father of her baby, I'll support her and the child financially." When she frowned, he added, "What? Did you think I *wouldn't*?"

"No, no... I, well, I didn't know what to think."

"Surely you didn't think I'd abandon my child. You know me better than that, Eve. I'd never do that." He could have added that he'd always wanted a child, because he had. He'd been envious of friends who had families. It was just that he'd never imagined having a child like this. When he'd thought about it, he'd seen a traditional family, with a wife he loved in the picture.

With Eve.

But the way things were beginning to look, maybe she didn't love him the way he'd thought. Maybe his feelings were one-sided. He hadn't imagined she was that good an actress, that she could have responded to him the way she had if she *didn't* love him, but maybe he was wrong. He hated to think so. Hated to think he would have to say goodbye to her again, and this time permanently. But he couldn't force her to love him if she didn't. And if it was fear holding her back, he couldn't force her to be brave, either.

No, the next step belonged to Eve.

And all he could do was wait.

Eve had never been so frightened in her life.

What was she going to do?

She had thought she'd have weeks to figure all this out, but Adam had forced her hand. Damn that woman, that Bethany. If she hadn't made her announcement, this showdown wouldn't have happened. Adam would have waited to ask her to marry him, and she would have been better prepared.

Then again, if Bethany hadn't released that statement, the twins would have been at the pier with them. And then what? Eve's own mother had taken one look at Adam and known he was the father of her grandchildren. What if the same thing had happened with Adam? What if he'd realized the truth and asked her directly if the twins were his? She would have had to tell him the truth.

Oh, be honest with yourself. You'd have had to tell him the truth regardless. That's why you've been so scared. That's why you attacked him the way you did. That's why you've tried to run away without facing this.

And once she had told him he'd have been so disappointed in her and so angry at the ongoing lie she'd perpetrated, he would have changed his mind about wanting her. Then she'd have had a different problem right now, one that was even worse.

What should she do?

She'd refused a ride back to the hotel with Adam, instead opting to call her own cab. She told Adam she'd see him when she returned to Crandall Lake and asked him to please not call her in the meantime.

Once she returned to her room, she phoned Bill. "Adam is going back to Texas. Please tell the twins I feel better and that I'm coming over in an hour. Have them pack a few things, including their bathing suits. I want them to stay here overnight."

"I don't think—"

Suddenly she was sick of him. Sick of everything. "You know, Bill, I really don't care what you think. I'm coming, and that's that."

An hour later, her cab pulled up in front of Bill's cottage. "Please wait," she told the driver. "I just need to collect my kids."

The twins were excited to see her. "I'm glad you feel better, Mom," Nathan said, hugging her.

"Me, too, honey. I didn't want to waste a day out here since I won't be here very long."

Natalie came in for her hug, and Eve looked up at Bill. "I'll have them back before dinner tomorrow night."

His smile was tight. "Have fun, kids."

Once the three of them were in the cab and heading back to her hotel, Eve finally relaxed. "I thought we'd spend the afternoon at my hotel. They have a great pool, and a really nice restaurant. We can have lunch there, you can swim this afternoon, and tonight we'll go see a movie or something, okay?"

"Yeah!" they chorused together.

"It'll be a good day," Eve said. But even as she made the promise, she wondered who she was trying to convince. Them? Or herself?

Adam couldn't get on a nonstop flight back to Austin until the next morning. Later, he'd never know what had made him decide to go to Eve's hotel and try to talk to her again, but that was what he ended up doing. If he'd thought to bring his guitar with him when he'd flown to LA, he probably would have simply stayed at his house and worked on his music, but he hadn't, and he couldn't stand sitting still. He didn't ask Luther to drive him, either. Instead, he took the Jag Austin had talked him into buying and drove over to her hotel himself.

When he rang her room and there was no answer, he walked over to the front desk and asked the girl on duty if she knew where Mrs. Kelly might be.

"Actually, I do, Mr. Crenshaw." She gave Adam her brightest smile. "She and her children went out to the pool."

Adam spotted them immediately. Eve, wearing a red bikini and huge dark glasses, lay on a chaise in the shade, and watched a group of four or five children playing some kind of water polo. Adam assumed her twins were part of the group. He knew she was going to be angry he'd come to the hotel after saying goodbye to her, but he'd figured he really had nothing to lose. He couldn't leave things the way they were when she'd left the pier. Besides, he'd forgotten to tell her about his visit with her mother and how Anna had encouraged him. Maybe if Eve realized her mother was in favor of them getting back together, she wouldn't be so afraid.

As he walked toward her, he was glad he'd changed into his Southern California disguise of baggy shorts, flip-flops, a beat-up T-shirt, big sunglasses and a baseball cap, because none of the other sunbathers seemed to recognize him.

In fact, Eve didn't take any notice of him, either. It was only when he sat on the chaise next to her and said, "Eve," that she turned to him.

It was almost comical the way her mouth dropped open. She immediately sat up. "What are you doing here?"

"I forgot to tell you something and I wanted to say it in person."

"You...you have to go. I can't talk to you here." She was looking at the kids, and there was panic in her voice.

What the hell was she so afraid of? "I'm not going anywhere."

"You have to!"

"Eve, calm down. Why are you acting like this?"

Before she could answer, one of the boys climbed out of the pool and walked toward them, dripping water everywhere. He was a slender youngster, but not scrawny. His hair was darkened by the water, but Adam imagined it was a medium brown. There was something about the way he walked that seemed so familiar to Adam. A second later, he recognized what it was. The boy walked exactly the same way Aaron walked. In fact, he looked a lot like Aaron had when he was a kid.

Eve seemed frozen as the boy said hi to Adam.

And then he smiled.

Adam felt as if someone had punched him in the gut when he saw the deep dimple in the boy's left cheek. *Holy shit!* For a moment, he couldn't say anything, but finally he returned the boy's smile. "You must be Nathan," he said, holding out his hand. "I'm Adam."

"Yeah, I know," Nathan said. His eyes were bright with excitement. "You and my mom are friends."

Eve had still not spoken a word.

Nathan turned around and yelled toward the other kids, "Nat! It's him! C'mon over."

A minute later, all four kids who'd been playing together came rushing to join them. They clamored around Adam, pushing each other to be the closest.

By now, Eve had recovered somewhat, enough to say, "Give Mr. Crenshaw some room, kids."

Adam studied the other children, and it was easy to see which one was Natalie because the only other girl in the group was older, with red hair and freckles, whereas Natalie looked a lot like Eve. When she saw him looking at her, she came closer and said, "I've been wanting to meet you, but my mom said we'd have to wait till we got back home."

Adam tried not to let on how rattled he was when he returned her smile. But those eyes of hers were the only confirmation he needed to show him he was right. Nathan and Natalie were his children. His and Eve's, not

Eve and Bill's. No wonder Eve had been so scared. No wonder she'd tried to avoid having him meet the twins.

All these years.

All these years she'd been keeping this from him.

This *huge* secret.

His heart was beating too hard as the knowledge sank in. He kept staring at the kids, even as he tried to behave normally, to answer some of the questions the children were firing at him.

Did Eve's mother know?

Did Bill?

Of course they did. They would have to. This must be why Eve had tried to get in touch with him twelve years ago. She must have found out she was pregnant and tried to let him know. And then, when she couldn't find him, she had married Bill instead.

Conflicting emotions warred inside him. He was angry she'd kept this secret from him all these years, but he was also sad for the pain he'd caused her—and for all the years he had missed out on while his children were growing up with another father.

If only Eve had tried harder to find him.

If only she'd called his mother, done something more.

But all the if onlys in the world wouldn't change the past.

Now the only question was, what was he going to do about the future?

Chapter Thirteen

Eve could hardly breathe.

Her worst nightmare had come true. She felt as if every person sitting around the pool must know her secret now. She knew this was ridiculous. No one could know. Maybe Adam didn't even know. Yet looking at her twins, she couldn't imagine he wouldn't see what she saw.

Nathan was his spitting image.

And Natalie's eyes were a dead giveaway.

Dear heaven. Of course Adam knew.

She couldn't look at him. Couldn't bear to see the condemnation in his eyes. Earlier today he'd said he loved her. He'd asked her to marry him. He'd shown her the most gorgeous ring she'd ever seen. He couldn't know how his words had thrilled her yet terrified her at the same time. She loved him so much. The days—and nights—they'd spent together in Austin had been some of the happiest of her life. She had wanted, more than anything in the world, to say yes, to say she'd marry him and make a home with him and their children.

But how could she say yes with this secret between them?

And now that he knew the truth, he would no longer want her.

Eve wanted to cry.

She couldn't look at Adam. She listened as he bantered with the kids, but the words meant nothing. All she could think was that there was no way to salvage this impossible situation. Her second chance to build something with Adam was finally and irrevocably over.

Adam felt as if someone had hit him with a sledgehammer. He wasn't sure what to do, whether to get up and walk away, go somewhere to calm down or stay and face Eve and let the truth finally come out.

Yet even as upset as he was, he knew he had to behave as if nothing was wrong because of the kids. They were all so excited that he was there. They weren't about to go back into the pool and forget about him. And he certainly didn't want any of them, but especially Nathan and Natalie, to realize something was seriously wrong. So it was imperative he act normally.

But what was normal?

Think! How *would* he act if this was a normal day? If he hadn't just found out one of the most important things in his life?

Normally, he would join them in the pool. Buy himself some time before having to talk to Eve. Deciding he could probably find a bathing suit in the hotel's gift shop or one of the other shops he'd noticed earlier, he said to the kids, "Why don't you all go back in the water? I'm gonna buy a bathing suit, then I'll come join you."

"You *will*?" This came from Nathan, who was so excited he was hopping from one foot to the other.

"I will." For the first time since the kids had come out of the pool, Adam turned to Eve. "If that's okay with you?"

She nodded. He wished he could see her eyes, but her glasses were too dark.

Twenty minutes later, wearing a navy suit and carrying a blue-and-white beach towel, his other belongings stowed in a canvas carryall he'd also purchased in the gift shop, Adam rejoined Eve. After dropping his stuff on the chaise next to her, he said, "Want to come in the water with us?"

"Maybe later."

But an hour passed, and she still hadn't joined them, and Adam knew she wasn't going to. He also knew it was time to say goodbye to the kids and get out of there, because the longer he stayed, the harder it was to keep pretending everything was fine. He knew if he didn't leave soon, he might lose it and say something to Eve, and this was not the time or the place to have that kind of confrontation. Not with the kids in hearing distance.

After promising the twins he would see them again soon, he climbed out of the pool. Walking over to Eve, he reached for his towel, dried himself off and said, "I'm taking off, Eve. I'm going back to the house, getting ready and then flying back to Crandall Lake. I may even go on to Nashville tomorrow. Depends. I need to talk to Austin and then to Bethany. Get that whole mess straightened out."

"Okay," she said in a small voice.

Part of him felt sorry for her, knowing she was as upset as he was, but the other part of him, the part that had been denied knowledge of his children for twelve years, wanted to lash out at her. Hurt her the way she'd hurt him. Because the truth was, if she had been brave enough to leave with him all those years ago, none of the rest of this would have happened. He would have been there when the twins were born. He would have had the past twelve years with them. They would *know* he was their father. "And you need to get some things straightened out, too, don't you?" he said. When she didn't reply, he hardened his heart. "When you get back home, we'll talk. Decide just how we're going to deal with this mess."

And then he left.

He didn't look back.

The rest of the day was difficult for Eve. All she could think about was the look on Adam's face when he'd realized the twins were his. She knew he was hurt, that he felt betrayed. And yet, how could things have been any different? If she'd gone to Nashville with him when they were kids, and then discovered her pregnancy, he would have had to do things very differently. He would have had to get a job and wouldn't have been able to keep making music, to keep pounding the sidewalks and haunting producers' offices. Adam Crenshaw and Version II wouldn't exist. And how happy would Adam have been if she'd been the reason he'd had to give up his dreams? Would they even be together now, twins or not?

Hadn't she given him the freedom and time necessary to achieve what he'd achieved? Hadn't she, in the end, been responsible for his success just as much as he was?

This, and many other thoughts, tumbled through her mind as she pretended to be enjoying the day with the kids. They were all excited, of course. Seeing Adam, spending time in the pool with him, had made their day and they couldn't talk about anything else.

Every word out of their mouths added to the pain in Eve's heart. How would they feel about her—and *him*—once they learned the truth? And learn it they would. Of that, Eve was certain. Adam would not be content to be the secret father. She knew him well enough to know that. He would want to be a part of their lives.

But no matter what he wanted, she knew Bill would be adamantly opposed. She really had made a mess of things. And no matter how she looked at their dilemma, it seemed that nothing but trouble lay ahead.

Austin stared at him as Adam told him about the twins.

"You're kidding."

Adam shook his head. "No, I'm not."

"You have eleven-year-old twins."

"Yeah."

"And possibly another baby on the way courtesy of Bethany."

"So she says."

"Jesus, Adam."

"I know. It's a mess, isn't it?"

"It's more than a mess. It's a damned circus."

Adam laughed mirthlessly.

"What're you doing to do?" Austin's hazel eyes, so like their mother's, shone sympathetically.

"Hell, I don't know. When I first realized Eve had concealed the truth about the twins, I was so upset I wanted to tell her off, make her suffer. But after I calmed down, I started to kind of understand. When she got pregnant, she was just a kid, Austin. I'm sure she felt desperate and scared out of her mind."

Austin nodded. "You know, if she *had* told you, you'd have had to support a wife and two kids and you'd have probably never had the kind of career you have now."

Adam nodded grimly. "I know."

"So do the kids know?"

"No. But I want 'em to. I want 'em to know I'm their father, not Bill Kelly." Adam sighed heavily. "But before I can do anything about the twins, I need to do something about Bethany."

"I figured that, so I've done some checking, and as far as I can tell, she hasn't seen a doctor yet."

Adam frowned. "You sure?"

"Positive."

"So she's basing her claim on a home pregnancy test?"

"I don't know *what* she's basing it on. You'll have to ask her."

"Nothing like the present." So saying, Adam reached for his cell phone and placed the call.

She answered almost immediately. "Well, well, well," she said. "Look who's calling."

"Don't act as if you didn't expect it," Adam said.

She chuckled. "You're right. I expected it. In fact, I expected it sooner."

"I was out in LA. I waited till I got back to Texas."

"Yes, I knew you were in LA."

"That's right. I forgot. You hired a PI to keep tabs on me."

"Yes, I did." She sounded smug.

"So, Bethany, let's cut to the chase. How far along are you and what do you want?"

"I'm three months along, according to my calculations, and I want you to acknowledge your role in the creation of this baby and to act like its father."

"According to your calculations. Does that mean you haven't seen a doctor?"

"I don't need to see one yet. I tested myself. Three times!"

"I need more than your word, Bethany. So once your pregnancy is confirmed by a doctor, and once *I'm* confirmed as the father, I'll take full financial responsibility."

"Only financial responsibility?"

"First things first. When I see the results of DNA testing, then we'll talk further."

"I have no intention of having amniocentesis, if that's what you're suggesting. It's too invasive and possibly dangerous."

"Austin tells me there are several noninvasive tests that can be done."

"I didn't know Austin was a doctor."

"He's done his research. He can make the arrangements for you."

"Excuse me? I see no reason for any kind of test at

this point. You'll just have to wait till after the baby's born. Now, I realize that's going to cramp your style, but—"

"Personally," he said, interrupting her, "I would think you'd want to prove your claim as quickly as possible. Because if you don't, that only reinforces my theory that you're lying, which is exactly how I'll tell my new publicist to spin our response."

"New *publicist*?"

"Sorry. Did I forget to tell you? You're fired."

"You're *firing* me?"

"Is that so hard to believe?"

"Won't the tabloids love that picture of you being vindictive?" she said sharply. "You sure you want that kind of publicity on top of everything else?"

"The publicity won't be targeting me. Not after I point out that you never saw fit to talk to me before springing your story all over the news. That you were obviously trying to do as much harm as you could, which means you forgot you still worked for me when you deliberately sabotaged me."

Austin was nodding his approval. He'd never liked Bethany.

Adam was tired. Tired of her, tired of the whole conversation, tired of everyone who'd let him down. So he ignored her sputtering protests and said, "I'm hanging up, Bethany. Let me know when you're ready for testing. Until then, we have nothing more to say to each other."

When Eve brought the twins back to Bill's the next afternoon, she quietly told him they needed to talk privately. So he walked outside with her, and she told him about Adam showing up at the pool the day before and what had transpired.

"So he knows," Bill said flatly.

"Yes. He knew the moment he met them."

"What does he intend to do about it?"

Eve shrugged. "I don't know. He wasn't happy with me when he left. And yes, he's leaving California. Might already be gone."

"I don't care whether he's happy or not. Legally, he has no standing."

"Bill…"

"He doesn't, Eve. The law says I'm their father."

Eve didn't want to make things worse, but he had to face facts. "Yes, right now that's true. But I never let him know about the twins, Bill. If he goes to court, he can demand his rights." She didn't add that Austin Crenshaw, who handled all Adam's legal matters, was one of the best lawyers around. Or that Adam had the financial resources to fight forever, if necessary.

"Have you told the twins?"

"No, of course not. I wouldn't do that without you being there."

"I suppose they were all excited to meet the great Adam Crenshaw," he said bitterly.

"They're just kids, Bill."

"And when they find out he's their real father…" His shoulders sagged, and he looked as if someone had kicked him.

Dear God. She'd hurt so many people. "I'm really sorry, Bill."

He stared at her. "You're not sorry. This is what you wanted to happen. So you can go off and play happy families together."

"I *didn't* want this to happen! It's the last thing I wanted." But was she being completely truthful? Hadn't she, deep down in her secret heart of hearts, wished she could tell Adam about the wonderful children they had created between them?

"I promise you, Eve, if he takes this to court, if he tries to push me out of the picture, I will fight him, and it will get ugly. You tell him that. Tell him to think twice about what he does. 'Cause I don't intend to go down easy."

When Eve returned to Crandall Lake two days later, Adam was gone. He'd texted her to say he was going to Nashville and would be away for a few days. That they would talk and decide what to do when he returned.

Eve was a wreck while he was gone. She told her mother everything that had happened, and although Anna was sympathetic, she had no advice to offer.

"It's a mess, Eve," she said. "I can't think how everyone is going to come out of this happy. Someone is bound to get hurt."

Olivia agreed. "I thought my situation with Vivienne was bad. But my life is a piece of cake compared to yours."

"Gee, thanks," Eve said wearily.

"Well, just sayin'."

The twins were oblivious, though. When Eve talked to them, they chattered happily. They were having a great time, they loved California, they were excited about meeting Adam and couldn't wait to see him again and this was the best summer ever.

Eve listened, her heart aching. They had no idea

what was coming. How their lives were going to be turned upside down.

If only she could do something. Anything. But she couldn't. All she could do was wait for Adam to come back.

But Adam didn't come back when he'd said he would. And she didn't hear from him, either. She did hear from Bill, who wanted to know what was going to happen, and she couldn't tell him.

"This is unacceptable," he said. "What is he waiting for?"

But Eve didn't know, and her misery and worry grew each day. She thought about calling Adam, but each time she started to, she changed her mind. She wasn't sure why, but she had this feeling that it was better not to push him, to just wait and let him call her.

Finally he did.

"I've had a change of plans," he said. "I'm not coming back to Crandall Lake right now. I'm going to stay here in Nashville for a while."

"But—" Eve stopped. She didn't know what to say. What did his decision mean? "I—I thought you wanted to talk."

"I need more time to think about everything before we talk. When will the twins be home again?"

"They'll be back the second week of August. They have to be. School starts the following week."

"Okay. Maybe by then we'll know how we want to go forward."

"You mean you're not coming back until then, either?"

"There's no reason to, is there?"

Eve closed her eyes. Fought the tears that threatened. His voice was so reasonable and so cold. He was making it so clear that he no longer loved her. Finding out about the twins had changed everything for him.

"Have you told the twins about me yet?" he asked calmly, for all the world as if he hadn't just broken her heart.

"No. I…didn't know if you wanted to be there…" Her voice trailed off. She didn't trust herself to say anything more.

"I've thought about that. I think you and Bill should tell them. Let them get used to the idea before they see me again. That might make everything easier…for all of us…don't you think?"

I can't do this. I cannot do this. "If…if you think so."

"I do think so."

He sounded so impersonal. As if she were a stranger. She wanted to weep. He hated her now. She wanted to ask what would happen with his mother, if Lucy would be going to Nashville, or what, but she couldn't. His distance, the way he was talking to her as if she were a stranger, wouldn't let her. She wanted to say, *Don't do this, Adam. Don't shut me out. Forgive me. Please forgive me.* But she couldn't say that, either. She couldn't say anything.

Somehow she got through the rest of the call without breaking down. Adam said he would keep in touch, let her know exactly when he was coming back. Then just before hanging up, he added, "If the twins, either one of them, want to call me, give them my cell number."

"I… Okay."

"Thank you. I'll see you next month."

Eve could barely function the rest of the day. And

that night, she cried herself to sleep, knowing this was only the first of many more lonely, tear-filled nights in her future.

At the end of July, Eve flew out to California again. She had been afraid Bill would fight her about telling the twins anything, but he surprised her, saying he and Missy had had several long talks about the situation, and she had pointed out to him how happy they were and how Eve deserved a second chance at happiness, too.

"I'm still not thrilled about having to tell the twins I'm not their birth father," he said, "but I know it has to be done."

Eve, who seemed to cry at the drop of a hat nowadays, got teary-eyed again. Bless Bill. Bless Missy. So Eve and Bill told the twins about Adam together.

Nathan squealed when he realized what they were saying. "Adam? Adam Crenshaw is our *father*!" His eyes were huge, his grin infectious.

Natalie's mouth dropped open and the color drained from her face. She seemed to be in shock. "Mom?" she said softly, moving closer to Eve. "Is it true?"

Eve took her hand. "Yes, darling, it is."

"But, Mom…" Natalie's eyes filled with tears.

With all her heart, Eve wished she could have spared her children this trauma.

The four of them talked for a long time. After putting little Will to bed, Missy joined them.

"Does this mean Will isn't our brother?" Natalie asked, her lip quivering.

"Of course he is," Missy said. "He'll always be your brother."

"Just like I'll always be your father," Bill said.

Natalie nodded, but her eyes were sad, and Eve knew her daughter was smart enough to know that nothing would ever be the same again.

Eve stayed in California for three more days before going home again, and by the time she left, the twins seemed to have absorbed this new fact of their lives without any more drama. Kids were resilient, it seemed. They'd even asked if they could call Adam and talk to him, and she'd given them his cell number, although she knew Bill wasn't happy about that, either. But he loved the twins enough not to make a fuss.

Her heart felt like a stone in her chest as she boarded her plane. She thought about her upcoming birthday, which was her thirtieth, and how everyone would be wishing her happiness.

Right now, she wasn't sure she'd ever be truly happy again.

Chapter Fourteen

It took three weeks of bad publicity and reporters hounding her before Bethany finally barged into Adam's office, glared at him and said, "You win, you bastard! I'm not pregnant, never was, and trust me on this one—I'm *thrilled* to not be having your baby!"

Then she picked up the guitar-shaped paperweight Adam's agent had given him and threw it at him. Adam caught the paperweight before it hit him, and gave her a hard look. "If I were you, I'd leave now. Before I call security and have you thrown out."

Bethany stared daggers at him for a few more seconds, then turned on her heel and stalked out, slamming the door behind her.

Adam took a long breath, then carefully set the paperweight back in its place of honor. "Good riddance," he said softly.

Now he could get on with his life.

The twins came home suntanned, filled with things to tell her and excited about starting fifth grade the following week. Both of them liked school, which had always made Eve happy, because she'd loved school. Natalie got better grades, but Nathan was a good student, too.

"Adam's coming back to Crandall Lake tomorrow," Natalie told her once they'd gotten through the first greetings. "He told me to tell you."

"Did he?" Eve kept her voice measured. "So you've been talking to him a lot?"

"I talk to him every day," Nathan piped up. "I call him when I'm ready for bed. He said he likes saying good-night to me."

Eve hated how absurdly weak she was, how the smallest thing could reduce her to a quivering, emotional mess. But the guileless way Nathan had conveyed this information, the way his eyes lit up when he talked about Adam, the way he didn't seem to understand every word was like a knife to her heart, had undone most of the serenity she'd managed to build the past two weeks.

"You're both calling him Adam," she finally managed to say.

"Yeah," Natalie said. "He said he understood it would be too hard for us to call him Dad."

Eve nodded. Calling him Dad would have destroyed Bill. She didn't know if Adam had considered Bill when he'd said this, but even if he hadn't, she was grateful.

"So do you think he's gonna move here to Crandall Lake now?" Nathan asked. He took a huge bite of the lemon pie Eve had bought earlier.

"I don't know," Eve said.

"Adam said we'd all talk about the future when he gets here," Natalie said.

That night, Eve resorted to taking a sleeping pill because she knew if she didn't, she wouldn't sleep at all. She was wound too tight. And tomorrow she would need all her strength, and all her wits about her, because she was determined to face Adam and hear what he had to say without going to pieces.

She might lose everything else, but she still had her pride.

Adam didn't sleep well. He was nervous in a way he hadn't been nervous in a long time. He knew why. He wanted something badly, and he wasn't certain he would get it. That was something else that hadn't happened in a long time, because ever since he'd had his first number one record, when Adam wanted something, it was handed to him.

He hoped his luck hadn't run out.

Because he wasn't sure he could be happy again if things didn't work out his way.

And there was no guarantee they would.

Adam called Eve at twelve thirty. "Have you had lunch yet?"

"Yes," she said.

"Are you at home or the office?"

"I'm working at home today."

"Are the kids there?"

"No, they're at my mom's house."

"Good. Can I come over? I think we should talk before the four of us meet."

"Okay. But give me thirty minutes."

Eve was shaking after they'd hung up. Once again, he had sounded so impersonal. *You can do this. You're strong. You can see him without falling apart, no matter what he says or does.*

She changed clothes, dressing carefully, wanting to disguise the fact she'd lost weight since last seeing him. White tapered pants, a bright coral print top and a coral headband. She used more makeup than she normally did, too, otherwise he might wonder why she was so pale. *Please, God, help me get through this,* she prayed. *Don't let me start crying in front of him.*

Her doorbell rang exactly thirty minutes after their phone call. Her heart caught at her first sight of him standing there. He looked wonderful, as always. Today he wore his uniform of jeans and a T-shirt, but it didn't matter what he wore. He had never looked bad to her.

"Hi," he said.

"Hi." He hadn't smiled, but he didn't seem angry. Or cold. Maybe they could eventually be friends. Maybe one day she could see him without it hurting.

"C'mon in," she said, standing aside.

He walked past her, and she shut the door. When she turned to face him, he had a funny expression on his face. She opened her mouth to say, "Let's go into the living room," but before she could, he reached for her hand.

"Eve…" Even his voice sounded odd.

She swallowed.

And then he pulled her to him and kissed her. Every single nerve ending in Eve's body responded as if they'd been touched by flame. The kiss went on and on, hungry and demanding. They both moaned, and kissed and kissed. It was a good thing he was still holding her tight when the kisses ended, because Eve's legs wouldn't have held her up otherwise.

"I love you, Eve," he said. "I love you. I don't want to live without you anymore."

"I love you, too," she cried brokenly. "I've always loved you."

"Can you forgive me for the way I've treated you the past few weeks?"

Tears slid down her face. "I already have. I—I know I hurt you."

"Yes. You did. But I understand why."

"I hope so."

"I still want to marry you, Eve," he said. "If you'll have me."

"Oh, Adam, more than anything, I want to marry you. I just don't know how it can all work."

He smiled then. A big, beautiful smile that made her heart leap. "We'll figure it out. As long as you love me, we'll figure it out."

"I do. I do. So much."

They kissed again. And again. And kept saying they loved each other. Finally, he reached into his pocket and took out the ring box. And this time, when he opened it, she let him put that magnificent ring on her finger. The sight of it there made her start crying again.

"Why are you crying?" he said, kissing the tears.

"Because I'm so happy. But I'm also scared."

"Don't be scared. Let's go sit on the couch and talk. I promise you, we'll work this all out."

Two hours later, they were still talking, but now they were in the kitchen and she was making grilled-cheese sandwiches with sliced tomatoes, because she'd lied when she said she'd already had her lunch, and he'd admitted he hadn't eaten, either. After devouring a couple of sandwiches apiece and discussing every possible scenario, they'd finally come up with the best solution they could manage.

Their plan was, as long as the twins were in school, Adam would base his day-to-day operations out of Crandall Lake. Bill and Eve's custody agreement would stay intact for the school year, with them switching weeks. When Adam had to travel, if Eve could and wanted to, she would come with him, and the twins would stay with Bill. During the summer, though, the twins would live with Eve and Adam, going wherever they went, except for when Bill took his family on vacation. If he wanted the twins with him then, they would be.

"I think this is fair, don't you?" Adam said.

"Yes," Eve said. "I do."

Adam had said he would keep both his Nashville home and his Malibu home, at least for now. They could decide later what they wanted to do with them in the future, depending on how well things were working out. He and Eve talked about building a new home in Crandall Lake, though.

"Somewhere on the outskirts, with some land," he said.

Eve smiled. It all sounded wonderful. Too good to be true, actually. She wondered if Bill would agree.

She knew he wouldn't be happy about the summers, but Adam had said he wouldn't press the legal stuff if Bill was reasonable about everything else.

"I won't even object to them keeping his name. Later, when they're old enough, if they want to take my name, I'd love for them to." He even said he wouldn't insist on making any kind of announcement about their parentage.

"People are bound to find out, though," Eve said. "The twins are dying to tell people now."

"Bill can't blame us for that."

But Eve wasn't sure about that. One thing she did know. She wouldn't be entirely happy until they'd talked to Bill and he'd agreed to their arrangement. *If* he agreed.

"I think your cousin Olivia is right," Adam said when she said this aloud. "You do borrow trouble."

At four o'clock, Eve called Bill and asked him if he could come over that evening. "Adam is back," she said, "and has a proposition for you."

"I have something to tell you, too," he said.

Eve frowned. That didn't sound good. Some of her happiness faded. What now?

But she could never have imagined what Bill was about to say. After he and Adam had warily shaken hands and the three of them were settled in the living room, Bill said, "Before we left California, my company offered me a permanent position in LA, and I want to take it."

"What?" Eve said, shocked. She'd never expected this.

"It's a terrific opportunity, more money and responsibility than I'd ever have if I stay here," Bill said.

"Missy's excited about it, too. You know her sister's in San Francisco."

"But the twins…" Eve said.

"I know. That's the only bad part. I thought maybe if you have them during the school year, I could have them summers and holidays."

"Summers and holidays!" Eve said. She looked at Adam.

"I have a better idea," Adam said. "Eve and I haven't had a chance to tell you yet, but we're planning to get married. We had talked about me making Crandall Lake my new base. But what if we live in California for the school year? I have a house in Malibu just sitting there empty. If we lived out there, you could see the twins on a regular schedule."

At first Bill seemed taken aback, especially when Adam went on to explain how he wanted the twins free to travel with them summers. For a while, Eve was afraid he was going to fight them, but after thinking about Adam's proposition for a few moments, he quit objecting. "I think it sounds like a workable plan," he said.

Eve met Adam's eyes. Maybe he was right. Maybe she *did* borrow trouble.

"Do you mean it?" squealed Nathan. "You're getting *married*?"

"And we're moving to California?" Natalie said. She was just as excited as Nathan, but in her new persona of an almost fifth grader, she obviously felt she had to act as if she wasn't.

Eve smiled. "Yes to both questions."

"And we're gonna live with you out there?" Nathan said.

"Yes. But you'll see your dad on weekends. And anytime during the week that you want to. And you'll stay with him when Adam and I have to travel."

"But what if our school is far away from where he lives?" This came from Natalie, who was always more practical.

"We'll figure all that out later," Adam said. "Maybe you'll go to a private school halfway between our houses."

"For now," Eve said, "let's just all be happy and... plan the wedding!"

This brought a delighted laugh from Natalie. She loved fairy tales and she especially loved weddings. "Can I be a bridesmaid?" she asked, gray eyes shining.

"A junior bridesmaid," Eve said, hugging her.

"When will the wedding be?"

"As soon as possible," Adam said, looking at Eve.

"Can I have at least a month to get everything ready?" she said, laughing.

"That long?" he said, looking to the twins for support.

"Yeah, Mom, that's too long," they both said.

Eve couldn't stop smiling. She was so happy. She couldn't believe how happy she was. God was good.

Two weeks later...

From the Facebook page of Adam Crenshaw
Posted by Amy Trenton, publicist for Version II

Here's a picture of Adam and his beautiful bride, the former Eve Kelly, flanked by their twins, Nathan and Natalie. Adam and Eve were married yesterday at City

Hall in Crandall Lake, Texas, where they both grew up. Adam says they'll have their marriage blessed in church at a later date, "but we didn't want to wait any longer to begin making our home together." The new Mrs. Crenshaw said she would keep everyone informed of their future plans and was looking forward to sharing Adam's life.

For the fashionistas among you, Eve's and Natalie's dresses, as well the dress of Eve's witness, her cousin Olivia Britton, are Vera Wang originals. Adam's tux was designed by Armani, as were those of his two brothers, Austin and Aaron.

Five hundred guests attended last night's reception honoring the new Mr. and Mrs. Crenshaw—see more photos below—which was held in the ballroom of the Crandall Lake Inn. After a short wedding trip to Paris, the newlyweds will make their home in Southern California and Nashville, with frequent visits to Crandall Lake in between.

Let's all wish the happy couple a long and beautiful life together!

* * * * *

ANNA CERMAK'S STUFFED CABBAGE ROLLS
(HALUPKI)

1 large head of cabbage
1 lb. ground beef
1 cup cooked rice
1/4 cup finely chopped onion
1 egg, beaten
1 tsp. salt
1/4 tsp. pepper
1 can condensed tomato soup
1 can sauerkraut
sugar
1 14-oz. can tomato sauce

Fill a large pot with salted water and bring to boil. Remove large outer leaves from the head of cabbage, thin the hard core and, using tongs, put the cabbage leaves, a few at a time, into the boiling water. Let cook until softened. Remove with tongs, let dry on waxed paper. Do this until you have at least eight to ten cooked leaves.

Combine beef, rice, onion, egg, salt and pepper with two tablespoons of the soup. Divide meat mixture among leaves and make rolls, then place rolls in roasting pan that has a thin layer of the soup spread over the bottom. Pour remaining soup over the rolls, top with sauerkraut and sprinkle a bit of sugar over the top (to cut the acidity and sourness of the kraut). Cover with foil and cook in a 325-degree oven for 1 ½ hours. Add tomato sauce, re-cover and cook another hour. Makes approximately eight rolls.

ANNA CERMAK'S PIEROGIES

For the dough:
3 cups all-purpose flour
2 eggs
½ teaspoon salt
Approximately 1 cup cold water

For the filling:
mashed potatoes
butter
salt

Mix all dough ingredients with enough water to make a medium-soft dough. Knead well, roll out until thin. Cut into squares to make approximately sixty. Place on each square a rounded teaspoon of the potato filling. Fold in half to make a triangle. Pinch edges well so filling won't escape. Drop in salted boiling water and cook until all pierogies rise to the top of the water. Then cook five minutes longer. When done, pour a small amount of cold water over the pierogies in a colander and drain.

Cooled pierogies can be frozen and used later or served immediately.

To serve

Slice several onions thinly, and cook in butter on medium heat in a skillet until caramelized and golden. Melt more butter when onions are done. Pour onions and melted butter over pierogies and serve.

Note from the Author

These recipes, combined with recipes from my aunt, Stella Sfara, and my good friend Christine Wenger, came from the kitchen of my own mother, Ann Duritza Sfara. I can personally vouch that they are delicious and loved by everyone in my family. *Bon appetit!*

To whet your appetite, coming in the next book of the Crandall Lake Chronicles series, Olivia's story, will be my mom's recipe for wonderful kolache, as well as one for her cabbage and noodles.

COMING NEXT MONTH FROM

H HARLEQUIN®

SPECIAL EDITION

Available April 19, 2016

#2473 FORTUNE'S PRINCE CHARMING
The Fortunes of Texas: All Fortune's Children
by Nancy Robards Thompson
Daddy's girl Zoe Robinson is unsure as to the claims that her father is a secret Fortune. But she's positive about her feelings for sexy Joaquin Mendoza. Still, can Joaquin, who doesn't believe in happily-ever-afters, find love with his Cinderella?

#2474 JAMES BRAVO'S SHOTGUN BRIDE
The Bravos of Justice Creek
by Christine Rimmer
Addie Kenwright is pregnant. And her dear old grandpa gets out his shotgun to make James Bravo do the right thing. James is not the baby's daddy, but he really wants a chance with Addie...

#2475 THE DETECTIVE'S 8 LB, 10 OZ SURPRISE
Hurley's Homestyle Kitchen
by Meg Maxwell
When Nick Slater finds an abandoned baby boy on his desk, the detective is taken aback—he's not ready to be a dad! So what should he do when his ex, Georgia Hurley, shows up pregnant? This journey to fatherhood is going to be quite the family affair...

#2476 HER RUGGED RANCHER
Men of the West
by Stella Bagwell
Ranch foreman Noah Crawford is afraid of opening his heart to love. So he wants to run for the hills when his boss's beautiful sister comes calling. But Bella Sundell has no intentions of letting him go...not when he could be the man of her dreams!

#2477 DO YOU TAKE THIS DADDY?
Paradise Animal Clinic
by Katie Meyer
Jilted by a bride he never wanted, Noah James's failed honeymoon turns into a second chance at love with lovely Mollie Post. But when he discovers he's a daddy, can Noah convince Mollie their summer fling could be forever?

#2478 THE BACHELOR'S LITTLE BONUS
Proposals & Promises
by Gina Wilkins
When single and pregnant Stevie McLane confides her baby secret in her friend Cole, she never imagines that he'd propose! This marriage of convenience brings the free spirit and the widower together for the love of a lifetime.

YOU CAN FIND MORE INFORMATION ON UPCOMING HARLEQUIN® TITLES, FREE EXCERPTS AND MORE AT WWW.HARLEQUIN.COM.

HSECNM0416

Joaquin nodded. "It was interesting. I saw a side of your father I'd never seen before. I have acquired a brand-new appreciation for him."

"That makes me so happy. You don't even know. I wish everyone could see him the way you do."

"Thanks for having him invite me."

Zoe held up her hand. "Actually, all I did was ask him if you were coming tonight, and he's the one who decided to invite you. He really likes you, Joaquin. And so do I."

He was silent for a moment, just looking at her in a way that she couldn't read. For a second, she was afraid he was going to friend-zone her again.

"I like you, too, Zoe. You know what I like most about you?"

She shook her head.

"You always see the best in everyone, even in me. I know I haven't been the easiest person to get to know."

Zoe laughed. Even if he was hard to get to know, Joaquin obviously had no idea what a great guy he was.

"I wish I could claim that as a heroic quality," she said. "But it's not hard to see the good in you. I mean, good grief, half the women in the office are in love with you."

He made a face that said he didn't believe her.

"But I don't want to share you."

He answered her by lowering his head and covering her mouth with his. It was a kiss that she felt all the way down to her curled toes.

When they finally came up for air, he said, "In case you're wondering, I just made a move on you."

Don't miss
FORTUNE'S PRINCE CHARMING
by Nancy Robards Thompson,
available May 2016 wherever
Harlequin® Special Edition books and ebooks are sold.

www.Harlequin.com

HSEEXP0416

HARLEQUIN®

A *Romance* FOR EVERY MOOD™

JUST CAN'T GET ENOUGH?

Join our social communities
and talk to us online.

You will have access to the latest
news on upcoming titles and special
promotions, but most importantly,
you can talk to other fans about your
favorite Harlequin reads.

Harlequin.com/Community

f Facebook.com/HarlequinBooks

y Twitter.com/HarlequinBooks

P Pinterest.com/HarlequinBooks

Love the Harlequin book you just read?

Your opinion matters.

Review this book on your favorite book site, review site, blog or your own social media properties and share your opinion with other readers!

THE WORLD IS BETTER WITH

Romance

Harlequin has everything from contemporary, passionate and heartwarming to suspenseful and inspirational stories.

Whatever your mood, we have a romance just for you!

Connect with us to find your next great read, special offers and more.

 /HarlequinBooks

@HarlequinBooks

www.HarlequinBlog.com

www.Harlequin.com/Newsletters

HARLEQUIN®

A *Romance* FOR EVERY MOOD™

www.Harlequin.com